WHEN MURDER COMES HOME

AILEEN & CALLAN MURDER MYSTERIES
BOOK ONE

SHANA FROST

Website: https://shanafrost.com

WHEN MURDER COMES HOME

First Edition.

Paperback ISBN: 978-93-5457-475-7

Large Print ISBN: 978-93-5659-567-5

Written By: Shanaya Wagh as Shana Frost

Copyedited by Laura Kincaid

Proofread by Charlotte Kane

Image on the cover by Vidarnm

BOOKS BY THE AUTHOR

You can find an entire (latest) catalogue on the website:
Shanafrost.com/books
Here's what you can read next…

Aileen and Callan Murder Mysteries
When Murder Comes Home
When Eyes Don't Lie
When Birds Fall Silent
When Red Mist Rises
When Old Fires Ignite
When Distilled From Rage
When Painted With Deceit

Banerjee and Muller Mystery Series
Smokes of Death Beer

To my parents.

Thank you for always believing in me.

SCOTTISH GLOSSARY

Bairn- Child
Bonnie- Beautiful
Clapshot- A traditional Scottish dish with mashed potatoes
and turnips
Eejit- Idiot
Grandwean- Grandchild
Lassie- Girl
Neeps- Turnips
Wee- Little

This book is written in English (UK)

PROLOGUE

The wind howled, its sound almost guttural. Dark grey clouds gathered over the inky sky, adding their sombre presence to the full-moon night.

Hadn't they always talked about creatures who woke up during a full moon?

The wind had picked up speed, almost pushing him back a step or two.

He wasn't sure if he'd ever make it. Maybe seeking shelter might be the right choice.

His life or the diamonds?

Remember, he warned himself, he'd taken an oath for the King. The diamonds...

He laid a hand over his heart. Was it to make sure it still palpitated?

He knew they'd be there. Those tiny shining crystals that neither he nor his ancestors could together afford. He'd tucked them against his heart when he'd vowed to his king, *'Je les protégerai de ma vie.'* (*I'll protect them with my life.*)

The skin over his heart felt the friction of the soft

1

pouch the diamonds sat in. His hands though – when he looked down at them, he could feel not a thing.

His fingers were frozen from the cold. His teeth were on the cusp of chattering.

Oh Lord, how would he survive the night?

The wind pushed him a few steps to the right. It was angry.

The full moon shone its sinister white light on the lone figure of a short, slight man, too ill-equipped for the weather.

He walked up a steep hill, on a muddy road, hunched against the brutal wind, his hand on his still warm heart, and hope in his heart – a wish – that no highwayman would chance upon him.

How far was Calais? Another day's journey perhaps – at least that's what he'd been told.

Yes, he was to hand off the diamonds to a man at Calais the next night. Oh, how relieved he'd be then. Only now, he was exhausted – he had travelled so far!

He groaned, giving in to his spasming muscles. His legs quaked; he stood on sheer loyalty to his King and continued.

The wind still assaulted him, the strange howl of an unnatural beast surrounded him and the night turned heavy with thick mist.

OH, HOW CALM THE NIGHT; NO STRONG WIND OR THE ROAR of a beast to shatter the earthly peace.

The coastal town was tranquil, fast asleep now.

A light, cold breeze danced through his hair. Anchored boats bobbed on the quay.

All the short, bone-thin man could do was wait.

His body jerked and halted, petrified, as a thick hand landed on his mouth; the other held a lethal knife to his throat.

'Diamants!' a gruff voice demanded.

The knife's razor-sharp edge glinted under a steady moonbeam.

The man's bony hands shook violently, but he somehow managed to remove a piece of paper from his pocket.

Another hard hand grasped the crumpled note. How many men had his captor brought along?

'Ah,' the accomplice grunted.

That must have been a cue, because everything immediately turned on its head.

It was quick. The mortal knife disappeared and in its place appeared a deadly hand. It clenched around the man's neck.

He knew something had gone wrong – vitally wrong. The King's diamonds would be lost and so would his life.

Another shudder; he felt the chill of fear run tremors through his body.

The soft brown bag that had been his companion for the last fortnight left the side of his heart.

Gone – the diamonds were gone.

A loud splash followed the weedy man as he crashed into the freezing water – silvery water, as cold as the dead.

CHAPTER ONE

I t had been a stupid thing to do! Who in their right mind left their job on a whim, put their house up for sale—which, mind you, they'd just paid the loan off on—and bid adieu to the city they'd always wanted to live in? All in a blink of an eye.

Only her.

No, Aileen reminded herself. It was time to be 'adventurous'. Her mind was so used to following a logical pattern that it was now in an ocean and didn't know how to swim.

Would she drown? Maybe she had bitten off more than she could chew.

No, no—she wasn't the old Aileen any more. She would never be *that* Aileen again.

Bummer, how long had she been driving? She had left the main motorway behind a long time ago. Had she seen another car on the road in the last hour?

But Aileen remembered all those summers spent at her gran's inn. She remembered the magical snow-splattered hills; the quiet burbling of the loch waters. Oh, how blue the loch was, a mirror reflecting the abundant cerulean abyss of the sky.

It was that dream she had recalled: those carefree summers where she had been adventurous. She'd chase rabbits and dip her toes in the cold waters of the loch when she'd been told not to.

Aileen sighed in awe at the pleasant scenery hurtling past her.

She was surrounded by rocks that stretched up to the sky. A gurgling stream zipped by the side of the road and right there was a ruined fortress: all the pieces that made the Scottish Highlands so bonnie.

The road turned narrower and raced away from the fortress. It went past hills, dense pine-filled forests and then, oh my! Aileen gasped.

In front of her was a large mass of deep cobalt water, as blue as the Scottish flag. And white snow sparkled on the mountains that stood tall and mighty behind the loch.

Home, her heart beckoned.

A smile cracked on Aileen's face, the frown that had settled there with self-doubt dissolving into pure joy, the stress that had taken residence in her body evaporating into the song of the Highlands.

Aye, she could hear the melody now. The wind whistled with the tune of a bagpipe playing ballads, as they seemed to have for aeons. These songs that scores of Scots had sung, danced, made merry or cried at.

A blue sign on the road announced Aileen had reached the end of the road. And hopefully a bonnie beginning in her life.

Aileen had reached Loch Fuar, the town with the cold lake.

❄

THE LONG SEDAN THAT DROVE THROUGH THE ANCIENT streets of Loch Fuar was caked in mud. The fact that it was long and a sedan told every passer-by that it wasn't local. There was no need for a number plate. It had disappeared behind the coated mud a long time ago.

The lass who stumbled out of the car had long brown hair. Some would say it was almost black. Her coat and shoes screamed city folk.

She stretched her legs as best she could. Grimacing at her sore muscles and then wincing at the look of her car, she blew out a breath.

A long way from home she was.

The tea shop's wooden door chimed open as Aileen rushed into the warmth.

The shop was filled with gusto. After all, it was late in the afternoon, time for some warming tea.

Aileen shuddered. She could do with a finger of whisky in hers. Her nerves were all over the place. Fish out of water made to mingle with people she didn't remember. Aileen's shiver turned into a moan as pain zinged across her back.

Perhaps she needed a warm bath to loosen her tight muscles.

'If it isn't MACKINNON!' a boisterous voice exploded in her ears. The tea room went quiet, all movement froze.

Aileen's heart began to thud wildly.

She searched for the voice in a room full of pink-faced —some heavily bearded—Scots who looked older than the Duke of Edinburgh.

One man stood and raised a beefy hand. 'Helped yer granny with the inn.' His voice held a strong Scottish burr. 'Remember ya as a wee lass running about. Look just like yer granny did fifty years past.'

Her poor heart had no chance—it was beating at such

a high rate, she thought she might collapse. Before she could react, Aileen lost her small hand in one of the smiling gent's.

Manners kicked in and in one exhale she muttered, 'Aileen—Aileen Mackinnon.'

'Aye!' This time it was an old Scotswoman who came up to her. 'Now I remember. You loved the shortbread I'd bake—never spared any for the other guests, remember?'

Aileen wedged her lips apart into a smile as polite as she could muster and felt the warmth of a blush tainting her cheeks. The last thing Aileen had come looking for was attention…

But this was a small town, and the Adventurous Aileen could talk to people.

As if experimenting, Aileen licked her lips.

'I remember you,' Aileen said in her simple dialect. She wished she had a burr too. That way she wouldn't stick out like a sore thumb.

Smiling at the people in the room, she tried retreating from all those kind, cheerful faces, but it was not to be. Instead, she ended up walking face-first into a hard chest.

'All grown-up, aren't ya? Such a bonnie lass…'

And so it continued. She was engulfed, thumped heavily on her back, pushed into a chair and stuffed with as much food as she could stomach.

It would have overwhelmed some. But to Aileen, it was a sign that she was indeed home. Even if that meant she'd had to combat her inner fears.

THE SKY WAS PAINTED IN A BEAUTIFUL LAVENDER SHADE, with a few bright stars shimmering like diamonds. The fresh air smelled sweet with the scent of wildflowers.

Aileen looked up at the clear sky and sighed.

She'd spent a busy evening with the local folk, laughing and talking. They showed no qualms about her being here. It had been so long now, more than a decade since she'd last been to Loch Fuar. And yet they'd been good to her.

How long had it been since she'd mingled and felt no urge to run for her life?

Aileen took a deep breath. Things were about to change because *Aileen* had changed. If sometimes she slipped back to her old ways, it would be fine. As long as she kept up being adventurous.

A bird sang a tune, a goodnight to his fellows, and Aileen lost herself in its sweet tune, tilting her head to glance towards her right.

Behind a stone fence, she patted with a smile, stood 'Dachaigh', her gran's inn.

Aye, this was her home now.

The old inn stood solitarily on a wee mound. Sturdy stone hid behind brilliant white paint, making it clean and welcoming.

Aileen let a laugh escape. Her grandmother had insisted the window frames be painted a distinct pastel blue. *It might attract bluer skies*, she'd joked.

Siobhan was that kind of a woman: twinkling cerulean eyes and hair gone white so long ago she hadn't a single brown strand left.

Aileen's grandmother had set up her inn five decades ago as a young widow. The short, yet independent mother of two had decided to fend for herself after her husband had died, so she'd travelled up to the Highlands with her sons and settled in a small town. The real estate was affordable for her, and Loch Fuar was a decent place to raise two strapping boys, so it was the best destination to set up her inn.

The innkeeper's chambers were on the last floor, Aileen recalled.

Her face split in an even wider grin. The inn had two storeys above the ground floor. From the outside though, the innkeeper's quarters couldn't be seen. They were stuck between the first floor and the slanting grey roof.

She'd loved trying to climb onto the roof from her granny's bedroom window. Siobhan had laughed at the attempt though her father had yelled at Aileen's dangerous antics.

The good old days.

Aileen looked at the inn again and took another steadying breath. She wished that joy would return to her heart.

With a jump in her step, humming a tune, Aileen made her way towards the entrance.

The wooden door, which had once seemed as gigantic as that of a castle's, now creaked open easily.

Aileen gasped. She had expected warmth, not rain! What a horrendous scene!

Three buckets were spread around the large reception area that led into what used to be a cosy drawing room. Water pattered languorously into the waiting buckets, like a ghost's laughter, while the plush sofas and cushioned chairs which were her grandmother's pride were covered in sheets of plastic.

What in the world?

Aileen's awkwardness withered from the blaze of her anger. Armed with a suitcase in her hand, she clomped over the plastic-covered floor towards the middle-aged woman sitting behind the reception counter, her face buried in her phone.

'Excuse me, Miss.' Aileen pressed her lips together and gestured at the lady.

The receptionist didn't even look up. She said, 'We need reservations first—no walk-in guests.'

Aileen hissed out, 'I'm Aileen Mackinnon, Siobhan's granddaughter.'

She lifted her face then, etched in what seemed to be a permanent scowl. 'Well, you can stay in whichever room you like. We don't have any guests.'

'Why don't we have guests?'

'Look around you, lassie.'

'Explain what I see.'

The scowling lady shrugged. 'We don't have any funds for repairs.'

'My grandmother is advised bed rest. She isn't here. So she can't know what the inn needs. You could have taken the initiative. Have you taken the trouble of asking Gran for funds?'

'Not my job,' came the answer.

'Well, it is your job to keep this place clean and bring in customers,' Aileen huffed. 'Tomorrow morning we'll work on this.'

'So you'll take over now?' The lady smirked. She hadn't bothered to introduce herself yet.

How could she charm customers with this attitude? The inn needed someone personable to keep guests returning every holiday.

Aileen decided tomorrow was soon enough to fight her battles. For now, she needed a good night's rest.

THE HIGHLAND MORNING HAD BEEN AS SCENIC AND pleasant as any Aileen remembered. She woke to the melody of birds, the sun shining bright through her window.

But the smile on her face promptly disappeared. Her gran's inn was in a state worse than any haunted house.

Aileen had been too exhausted to remark on the state of her mattress or her room last night. She sincerely doubted it had even been cleaned since its last guest had departed.

And now the larder, oh God's teeth! The entire larder was stocked with tinned food. Food that had expired a year ago. The entire thing stank of vomit and a cesspit mixed together!

Aileen gagged.

Her feet thundered on the stone floor and then over the wooden stairs as she burst out the front door.

Without skipping a beat, she jogged to her car and made her way to the main town. It was high time someone got the messages.

The rough road wound around tall trees, before crossing a buzzing stream. The city sedan tumbled over a short stone bridge. Nothing stirred except for the breeze weaving through naked tree branches.

Quaint Loch Fuar may be—boring it wasn't.

The dried foliage opened to reveal gigantic mountains, proud and mighty under the fresh pastel sky. Clouds in all forms and shapes decorated the blue gulf.

It was as if an artist had painted this masterpiece: 'The Beginning of Spring'.

A few short minutes later, small stone cottages began dotting the greenish landscape. Just looking at this view made Aileen feel as if she'd been transported back in time.

One cottage was alive, its chimney busily huffing out smoke, and as she drove past, Aileen smelt freshly baked bread through her open car windows.

These brick houses had probably stood here for ages. How many happy memories did they hold in their walls?

The narrow winding road opened up into a junction of sorts. Here, there were a few people strolling about.

It was the busiest place in Loch Fuar, as busy as Edinburgh's back alleys in the wee hours of a winter morning.

A cluster of three ladies stood, laughing and jesting with each other, while young children marched their way to school. They were primly dressed in uniforms, even though a few of their uniform skirts had muddied hems.

Scattered around this junction were all the essential shops: the grocer's, the butcher's, the baker's, a general merchandise store, and a handyman's shop.

Aileen had no time to waste. She quickly bounded towards the bakery. If memory served, the inn had bought bread here every day for the past fifty years.

The mouth-watering smell of bread tickled her nose, and her stomach growled, demanding breakfast.

'How are you this morning?' A cheery red-headed lad beamed at her from behind the counter.

'Oh hello! Fine weather, isn't it?'

'Aye! What would you like?' He waved a hand to indicate the stacks of bread-loaves.

Aileen hesitated. Would this be too intrusive?

'Well, I wanted to know how many loaves you supply at Dachaigh every morning.'

'Dachaigh? You mean the inn?'

Aileen nodded.

'We don't sell our bread to them anymore…'

That perked up Aileen's curiosity. She choked her doubt and continued, 'Why's that?'

The lad considered for a while and then leaned in as if to let her in on a secret.

'Have you seen the looks of that place? If it wasn't for Siobhan, the police would've shut the place a long time ago!'

Goosebumps appeared on Aileen's hand when the door jingled. A woman, barely five feet tall, walked in.

As if it was the actual police, Aileen! She rebuked herself.

The woman's cat-like green eyes twinkled with unfiltered exuberance, her cheeks flushed pink, and an aura of energy beamed from her and settled throughout the bakery. Her smile was brighter than the sun.

'I heard but… Aileen Mackinnon in the flesh!' She rocked enthusiastically in place.

Aileen's heart palpitated. She wasn't yet used to how gossip worked in Loch Fuar.

At Aileen's confused look, the woman bobbed her head and continued, 'Your gran always spoke about you. She doted on you, showed me all the pictures too. Are you back to fix the old inn?'

'Um, aye…' Aileen was unsure what to say, but she didn't get a chance to offer anything more before the lady spoke again.

'The innkeeper is a rude nut! Hope you fired her.'

When Aileen shook her head solemnly, the woman turned an exasperated set of eyes on her. 'Well, you should! What are you waiting for?'

Swatting a hand at the air, she continued, not waiting for a response, 'Don't worry a bit now, love. You see this entire town has your back. Say the word and we'll all be down there, mopping and cleaning up the place. Siobhan is ours. She treated my husband and his friends like hers when they were bairns.'

Aileen grinned, her fondness for her grandmother shining through. Siobhan was a grandmotherly woman when she wanted to be. But Aileen remembered that one time an awry guest had tried to sneak out an old bedside lamp. Her grandmother's wrath had been enough to scare the ghosts from all the Scottish castles combined!

'My grandmother is that sort of a woman. The bed rest the doctor suggested makes her restless—more so day after day,' Aileen managed finally.

It looked like the lady had run out of steam. She panted for a while, sucking in gulps of air, giving Aileen the chance to study her. With her wild red hair and pink cheeks, she looked similar to the lad behind the counter, though she was older—in her mid-thirties.

Having finally caught her breath, she flashed an energetic smile at Aileen—then, before Aileen could deflect, the woman engulfed her in a ferocious hug.

'Isla McIntyre,' she announced finally. 'I forgot to introduce myself! I'm so excited to meet you.'

Aileen filled her lungs with much-needed air when the woman let her go. It had been a tight hug! Random conversation and now hugs? Aileen shivered slightly. She'd never get used to this friendliness!

'Isla, have you—' a gruff voice approached with slow heavy footsteps.

'Ah, the talk of the town.' The tall yet broad man pointed a finger at Aileen. 'Mackinnon, the loved yet absent grandwean.'

Aileen groaned internally. Was there one person who didn't know who she was?

His heavy footsteps thudded on the stone floor, and Aileen noticed that, despite his sure footing, his gait wasn't regular.

A pair of eyes—electric blue mixed with some grey—assessed her. He wore black trousers with a black leather coat. His equally soot-black hair was neatly trimmed, almost in a military cut.

Holding out a calloused hand, he gripped hers and flashed a smile that felt almost mocking. 'Callan Cameron, I'm the detective inspector.' Pointing a finger at the door, he raised an eyebrow. 'Have you got a licence plate under all that…?' He frowned at her car through the shop window. 'Muck?'

Isla chirped in, 'Oh, Callan, don't scare the lass.' She turned to Aileen. 'He's a regular, here for a cup of coffee and a pastry. Why you can show her around sometime. There's no crime in Loch Fuar…' she teased Callan.

He flashed another smile. 'Now that's stretching it a bit too far. Only this morning Ms McHugh was complaining about her neighbour helping himself to some apples from her tree.'

'Oh, that old woman—always complaining she is!'

Callan tapped his card at the till and plucked his pastry and go-cup. 'Have a good day. You find your licence plate through all that mud. Stay safe, especially you Lowland folk,' he dismissed Aileen.

That got Aileen's blood boiling. She wasn't from the Lowlands! She'd grown up in the Highlands!

'I'm not…' she flustered but the annoyingly rude inspector was already gone.

CHAPTER TWO

Adventurous, that's what the past week had felt like.

Isla, as she'd insisted Aileen call her, had been serious about the entire town pitching in to help. That same evening she'd sent her nephew, the lad who'd greeted Aileen in the bakery, along with a few of his class-mates to lend a hand.

Before their arrival, Aileen had made a detailed list of what needed to be fixed. She shuddered even thinking about it.

The lads had helped her clean the guest bedrooms and dispose off the soiled bedsheets.

So appalled at the condition of the inn was she that the first thing Aileen disposed of—even before the stinky food —was the snooty innkeeper.

However, her happiness at ridding Dachaigh of its former innkeeper was short-lived. Even if she was as friendly as a jail guard, she'd at least known a thing or two about running an inn.

You are an accountant, Aileen reminded herself for the

thousandth time that week. She could take inventory and figure out the expenditures that ate into profits, but running an inn?

Aileen sighed ruefully at her self-doubt.

Wasn't this precisely why she'd left her former life behind? She chided herself—it was time to be spontaneous and courageous. The new Aileen didn't second-guess herself. No, she was a confident woman who embraced spontaneity.

More determined than ever, Aileen clambered down the stairs into the disastrous reception area—and took an involuntary step back.

Somehow the tall, muscled figure of Detective Inspector Callan Cameron in worn jeans and workman's boots suited the unruly plastic-covered reception area.

'Dachaigh was very different the last time I came down here,' the inspector observed with a judgemental frown.

CALLAN REMEMBERED MAKING A STOP AT DACHAIGH WHEN he'd first returned to Loch Fuar. The grandmotherly Siobhan had embraced him and cooked a warm, sumptuous meal as a welcome back gift.

It was her spirit that had kept this place going over the years, and this was more evident than ever given the way Dachaigh was falling apart.

He'd only heard the rumours after Siobhan had left for the nursing home—everyone had gossiped about how the innkeeper was more like the gatekeeper to Hell.

It was a good thing Aileen had fired her, though Siobhan's granddaughter seemed more lost than in control of the situation.

Callan studied the pitiful state of the inn and then the

figure of Aileen Mackinnon. She barely looked any better —the bags under her eyes made her look like a corpse in denim overalls.

Isla had subtly hinted every time he'd gone to get his morning coffee about the inn needing a hand for repairs. She'd also deliberately let it slip how Aileen was working tirelessly to get the place up and running before spring had finished blooming. Her interfering intention had been to sneak a date for her new city friend.

Callan dismissed those comments for what they were— pesky interference. But he was intrigued enough to drop in and maybe get a rise out of the prim and proper Aileen Mackinnon.

'HOW MAY I HELP YOU?' AILEEN ASKED AS POLITELY AS SHE could. The last thing she needed was an assessment by the police—Inspector Cameron in particular.

She couldn't put a finger on why, but he irked her, enough to make her forget about her self-doubts and personable manners.

Callan made a show of assessing the plastic covers before turning that gaze on her. 'You know, most people wouldn't travel to a small town in one of the coldest regions of the Highlands to run a dilapidated inn.'

Aileen raised one shoulder with an air of superiority but filled with hollow confidence. 'Well, I did and Dachaigh wouldn't be like you see it now—it'll be the best it's ever been.'

'Everyone here thinks Siobhan ran it best.'

Aileen folded her hands across her chest. 'You haven't seen my way yet.'

The inspector shrugged. 'Isla sent me here to ask if ye

need help fixing the leaks. I have a few friends willing to help this weekend.'

'Nah, I've got it covered.' Aileen couldn't possibly acknowledge that she hadn't a clue what to do about the leaks. Especially to this man who was waiting for her to make a mistake or worse fail—badly.

What a snob! Hadn't he just enunciated his thoughts about her: a city girl who knew not a thing about town life? Well, the joke's on him, Aileen thought: she learned well and learned quickly.

MAYBE SPENDING SUMMERS IN A TOWN WAS DIFFERENT FROM residing in one as an adult and innkeeper.

Stepping inside the handyman's shop had been a mistake.

The brawny yet friendly man behind the cash register had asked Aileen what she needed to fix her inn.

'We haven't got our stock of the claw hammer yet. I can send it over to the inn if ye like,' he informed her.

Aileen had no clue what a claw hammer did or what it was used for. She'd checked a YouTube video or two on fixing a leaking ceiling. They said she needed a drill, but the inn didn't have any sort of equipment on hand, hence this fateful trip.

Aileen blushed a little. That morning she'd climbed onto the ladder and poked the sagging ceiling with a long screwdriver, the only one left in the supply closet. At least that's what the internet had told her to do. Damn the internet!

No one specified that the entire thing might collapse on her head, leaving an evil hole in the ceiling! She'd been completely drenched!

Hadn't it been sheer luck the water was from a fresh-water pipe? The last thing Aileen wanted was to stink like a dunghill, and even though the reception area of the inn was flooded... She'd fix it.

Aileen cleared her throat and approached the man. His smile reached his kind eyes. So she dared. 'Er, um, you see I need some minor help with the leaks,' she began as bravely as she could.

'Ah, aye, Isla told me about it. Isla's my wife. That place is falling apart! I expected you'd hire someone to fix it up.'

'Oh... I... Ah...' If Isla knew, her miserable failure would soon be the talk of the town. Aileen cringed at the thought. With embarrassment flushing her cheeks.

Adventurous?

'My partner'll be along anytime now. Maybe I can come down and assess it for you?'

Aileen swallowed her pride. 'That would be very helpful.'

'Ah, Aileen, this doesn't look too good.'

She didn't say a word.

'Well, don't worry. I'll get the troops assembled and at work by... Do you have the necessary permits?'

Aileen shut her eyes and cursed her stupidity. Permits! How could she have forgotten permits!

Daniel held up his hand. 'Don't worry. I have a friend, who knows a friend in the council. We'll sort this out... Aye.'

With Isla and Daniel's help, Aileen sorted out the permits and a week later, got them approved. Daniel was at her door with a bunch of people armed with tools and equipment to set her roof to rights. And with that he'd also be fixing the old plumbing. And the reception area… And the rooms.

Isla's company kept her entertained through those days. She could speak someone's ear off. But her commentary helped acquaint Aileen with Loch Fuar's town dynamics. And Isla's own past.

'When I came over from Stirling, I didn't have a clue what to do with a broken light! That's how I met Daniel.' She said, helping Aileen clear out the soiled food cans.

'Oh, didn't Callan visit you? He's handy with a hammer—helps Daniel out sometimes. They're best mates.'

That meant he'd find out about her situation any day, if he didn't already. Aileen winced. He'd surely gloat for a while. But mistakes were stepping stones to success, she reassured herself.

'Um, I wasn't sure he'd know anything. He's a cop, not a—'

'Oh, he's a good man. And don't worry, between them, the inn'll be good as new before you know it!'

And thus days tumbled into weeks. The *dreich* days gave way to sunnier ones. As nature bloomed with spring, Dachaigh came into itself.

Daniel's team—Callan included on the weekends—repaired jammed windows, leaking pipes, chipped tiles, worn wallpaper, peeled paint and fixed the creaky furniture.

Apart from the cost of materials, all Daniel had asked in payment was a daily lunch for him and his men for the duration of their work at the inn. That was one thing Aileen could do very well—she was a decent cook and an amateur baker.

Isla assured Aileen it was her cooking that brought so

many helpful hands to Dachaigh, and it was true that everyone had complimented her on her cooking. Everyone except Inspector Cameron. He was a rude nut. Even if he helped Daniel out and laughed with the others, he had an aloof air about him. Aileen pushed her frustration at him to the side—how did it matter what he thought?

In just over a month, a new website announced that the Dachaigh Inn at Loch Fuar was open to guests once more, waxing lyrical about the incredible views from the inn's rooms: tall snow-clad peaks, green grasslands, and the shimmering blue Loch Fuar in the background kissed with a breeze as refreshing as melodies of birdsong.

A week after that, Aileen had her first ten customers booked. They'd all be here in the last week of April.

Fantastic!

The new Adventurous Aileen couldn't wait!

CHAPTER THREE

The morning of 29th April arrived with magic frolicking in the air.

Birdsong danced around the old cottages, wafted through tall trees heavy with cheerful blossoms and settled on the sleeping town of Loch Fuar at the crack of dawn.

Isla was up before the birds, excited for Dachaigh and Aileen.

Baking had always been her passion. That was before leaving the big town she'd been born and raised in. Now baking had become a beloved profession. It was the way she made her mark in this world, spreading joys with lip-smacking breads and pastries.

Isla hummed to herself as she thought about her coming to Loch Fuar in search of something amiss in her life. She remembered how at home the locals had made her feel.

Smiling, Isla measured out the flour and got to work. She had to be as quick as she could this morning. Aileen depended upon her to provide the bread.

The new innkeeper at Dachaigh was as green as the meadows in spring. Some would find her naivety a fault, and maybe it was. The coming days would tell if Aileen Mackinnon had inherited her grandmother's genes…

Isla knew just how it felt to be an outsider. Thus she'd decided she would help the pretty young girl out. So what if she made a friend in that process?

And it didn't hurt if this friendship helped get her some extra business from the inn, did it?

A couple of hours later, when the earliest risers in Loch Fuar stirred from the sleep of the innocent, Isla was armed with fresh loaves, cookies, cakes and scones.

She packaged some up for Dachaigh, ordered her sleepy-eyed nephew to guard the fort, and whizzed off in her car, heading straight for Aileen's inn.

It was time for the guests at Dachaigh to arrive. She couldn't wait to see what they were like.

Ten guests? Aileen almost bit her nails in worry. How was she to manage?

She'd never entertained ten guests for supper! And now here she was taking in paying guests at her gran's inn!

The tips of her fingers were a better bet than her dilapidated nails. Aileen gnawed on them instead. Her nerves were close to combustion. She'd given herself so many pep talks today, she'd lost count.

Perhaps they'd hate Dachaigh and ask for a full refund. How would she scrape together the money to repay them? She'd used it all for the renovations and the website.

Confidence.

Adventure.

Those two words were the only reminders she needed. She would not doubt herself.

Squaring her shoulders, Aileen picked up her detailed list. Lists could always be counted upon.

It took her an hour to check the bedrooms. She made sure there were bath towels, hand towels, bathrobes, and a scented candle in every bedroom, along with a set of necessary complimentary toiletries.

Another run through and the bedrooms were ready. She then scoured the reception area, now warm and cosy with not a hint of unwanted moisture or dirt.

A satisfied smile graced her lips. The reception area now opened to the charming drawing room. The cream walls added a hint of elegance, and the rustic walnut wood furniture was a reminder of home. The windows offered stunning views of Loch Fuar in the distance and the mountains beyond it.

Aileen had brochures ready for her guests, along with tourist maps, in case they needed any information about the locality.

Armed with a clipboard, her dark hair tied up in a bun, Aileen frowned at the ceiling.

That was how Isla found her.

'Now what's wrong with it?' Isla asked, pointing at the ceiling.

Aileen jumped. 'Isla!' Laying a hand over her heart, she said, 'Oh, it's nothing.'

'Excited?'

'Aye!' *And terrified out of my skin*, Aileen thought.

It could be an adventure or it could be a disaster, but Aileen decided she'd handle it just like she'd handled the last few weeks: with her chin up!

❄

JUST WHEN THE CUCKOO CLOCK IN THE DRAWING ROOM chimed the tenth hour, a black Land Rover pulled up and circled to the inn's parking lot.

Aileen twiddled her thumbs. This was it, she told herself. The journey begins.

Like a well-rehearsed dance, the doors on either side of the car opened at an angle slightly greater than forty-five degrees and a tall lean gentleman stepped out from one side. He had on a pair of goggles, which looked as sharp as his chiselled jaw, and his hair was painstakingly pulled back using a thick coating of hair gel. The crisp blazer he wore over a polo shirt seemed too fancy for a laid-back town-like Loch Fuar. Besides, his shoes were Oxfords – hardly apt for the Highland weather.

He gave a cursory glance at the inn, swiftly clicking the car's door closed behind him, then, with purpose in his stride, he walked like a panther towards Dachaigh.

On the contrary, the other gentleman who hopped out of the car was short and had a generous belly. He wore a pair of dark goggles too but hid the better part of his small face beneath a hat.

A sharp blazer over a polo shirt seemed to be a standard issue for these two, though unlike his companion, this gentleman had paired the ensemble with slip-on shoes. So unlike anyone she'd met in the town before.

Didn't most tourists take efforts to look less tourist-like?

The second man noisily clomped up the mud road towards the inn.

Aileen positioned herself behind the reception counter, her hands primly folded on the table and split her face in a smile.

It all felt real now. Her first customers were here.

'Dachaigh Inn?' a posh, heavily accented voice asked. It suited the tall man before her.

'Aye! How can I help you?'

A diamond glinted at the man's right ear. He looked at her down his pointed nose as he reached into his wallet, showing off an expensive watch. He had an air of superiority about him.

The door had barely clicked behind him when it swung open again and the shorter of the two men pattered in. Pulling the hat from his head, he revealed a balding scalp.

'Dachaigh at last!' He smiled sincerely at Aileen.

The subtle fragrance of a floral perfume wafted through the air.

Extending a ring-studded hand, he introduced himself. 'Jean Beaulieu. This is my husband, Louis Legrand.'

Aileen switched her smile from a polite one to a friendly one. What a pair! Apart from the clothes, they seemed to have nothing in common.

'I'm Aileen.' Both men had a distinct accent. 'Did you come from France?'

'*Non, non*. It's our country of birth. Now we live here but the accent is hard to... Shrug off.'

Legrand hadn't uttered another syllable. He continued to look displeased.

Aileen checked her list. Ticked their names off.

'If you could please fill in your details?' She handed the register over.

Legrand ignored the pen she offered and pulled out a shiny golden fountain pen. Aileen almost gasped out loud. A solitaire glistened on the pen's nib.

In clean cursive, he penned down their details. His husband had wandered off into the drawing room.

Beaulieu re-entered holding the complimentary lemonade Aileen had placed in a jug by the sofa set.

'Fresh!' He sipped at it. 'Louis, you must try.' He pointed to the jug in the drawing room.

Legrand gave him a brisk nod. 'What of the luggage?'

Aileen flustered a little, not sure what to say. Didn't guests haul their luggage themselves in an inn?

'Um, er, I'll get it for you!'

He nodded, holding out a key. 'You know where the car is.'

She had been dismissed.

Huffing at her guest's rudeness, she approached the slick car. The boot opened to reveal three large suitcases! Three for a weekend-long visit!

Struggling for breath, Aileen stumbled over the last suitcase as she got it indoors. It felt like they'd stuffed their luggage with rocks!

Now, these bags had to be carried a storey up.

Aileen sent up a quick prayer for strength.

She handed off the room keys to Legrand, informing him that she'd place the luggage up shortly. Beaulieu gravitated towards the windows, enchanted with the view.

'*Magnifique*,' Beaulieu exclaimed, slipping into French as he cheerfully pointed out something in the distance.

Mr Louis Legrand hadn't let out a single appreciative interjection. After a cool assessment of the drawing room, he subtly dragged his husband upstairs.

Aileen remained at the reception desk, twiddling her thumbs and biting her lip. Her first guests had given opposing reactions. What did that mean?

Did they hate it? Was Beaulieu being kind? Perhaps they—

From afar, a hoot from a car broke through her self-doubt.

A rental van hobbled towards the inn then rattled to a stop right at the gate. The left-hand-side door opened and an energetic flurry with red hair popped out of it.

'Oh, Dave, look at the view!' The red-haired lady's voice held excited jubilance.

She rounded the vehicle and crushed 'Dave' into a tight hug. The man looked flustered, barely catching his wife when she'd flung herself at him. His left leg was stuck in the car.

Aileen left the two of them to their own devices.

A few short minutes later, the front door opened. The red-haired lady who'd been bubbling with joy hopped in. Her husband followed, blushing hard.

He walked up to the counter, almost tripping over his legs. A pair of stubby hands latched onto the wooden table. His eyes were beady and looked a little lost.

'Smiths, we are.' He cleared his throat. 'That's my wife, Martha and, um, I'm Dave.'

Lost and unsure, his shoulders sagged a bit as his gaze flittered around the inn.

Martha had wandered into the drawing room. Now and then she exclaimed at the beautiful landscape: it started with the 'magical' loch, then the 'awe-magnificent' mountains and then went on to the sky and the birds.

'It's my birthday this weekend. We're here to spend it together.' The husband blushed again.

'That's wonderful! We have a fantastic bakery in the town. Would you like a birthday cake?'

Isla would love to bake a cake for him – Aileen was sure of it.

'Er, yes, that'd be brilliant.' He filled in the register with the ordinary pen she offered, unlike Legrand.

This couple seemed normal enough. Despite the contrast in their moods and energy levels, they fit in perfectly.

Martha danced back to her husband's side.

'You have the most magnificent estate! Oh, Davy, you're about to have the best birthday ever!'

She peered over her husband's shoulders. 'We should get our luggage!'

'I'll do that.' With that, Dave Smith escaped.

'He's such a dear! Say, what are the touristy activities hereabouts?'

Martha and Dave were a young couple, just crossing the thirty mark, Aileen predicted. They were smartly dressed for the Highland weather: thick boots, jumpers, jackets, scarves and trousers, ready for a hike.

Aileen took out her neatly designed and printed leaflets and spread them out on the table between them. She'd always been good at creative projects like these in school.

'This is the Loch Fuar. It's wonderful. You can't miss it. If the weather holds, you'll be able to take a picnic there. But please do be careful – the road down is a little... Tricky.'

'Maybe on Dave's birthday. Can we swim in the loch?'

'I'm afraid that's not permitted. You see Loch Fuar is called that for a reason. It's frosty, throughout the year, even in summer.'

'That should be a welcome sight in summer.'

'Um, it's uncannily cold there, Mrs Smith.'

'Oh, I sense there's a mystery there...' She waved a dismissive hand. 'What else can we get done?'

Aileen suggested some other options to the energetic Martha Smith: she could check out the town, they could go on a hike up the hills or perhaps visit the local museum. The hike was well received. Apparently, it was something right up their street.

At least they were courteous enough to carry their luggage upstairs, and they chattered happily as they trudged the two small suitcases up.

Peering outside, Aileen groaned. Despite their helpfulness, they'd left the van parked right in front of the inn!

A rugged car pulled up behind the rental. It had been a while since the road passing Dachaigh had seen so much traffic. But this car Aileen ruefully recognised as belonging to Detective Inspector Callan Cameron.

He strode up the three stairs and inside the inn.

'You let the guests park on the road now? Got to charge ye for breaking traffic rules. This isn't a private road,' he began without a preamble.

This was the last thing Aileen needed.

She raised her chin in defiance. 'I was about to ask them to park their van in the appropriate area.'

'And the luggage? Don't they know they've got to take it up with them?' Inspector Cameron pointed towards the French couple's bags behind the reception desk. His husky voice mocked Aileen.

Right – he thought she was just a city girl, no good in a Highland town. Miffed, she trolleyed the first of the huge suitcases to the staircase.

Hoping her irregular workouts would pay off, she lifted the first suitcase. Heavy footsteps followed her as she placed one trembling leg in front of the other.

It was sheer willpower that had Aileen hold her own. She nearly tumbled over a stair at one point, and her hands were shaking, but she carried on.

At the landing, the suitcase thumped on the floor. It was joined by another. This one gracefully placed beside the suitcase she carried.

'You've got muscles,' Callan said, smirking. Aileen seethed, clearly, he'd assumed she couldn't manage on her own.

'It's an innkeeper's job to keep guests satisfied.' It came out like a well-rehearsed phrase. She'd repeated it in her head a couple of times since Legrand had so rudely brushed her off that morning.

Callan laughed. He could mock all he wanted. Aileen knew he'd predicted she'd run back to the city a week after moving here, overwhelmed by the Highland way of life.

A burning fire to defy him blazed in Aileen's stomach. She'd prove that snarky inspector wrong!

'Don't the police have important matters to get to?' she asked coldly.

The polite 'get out' seemed to bring him out of his thoughts.

'Well, we do have the occasional theft. In a town where there's been no murder for decades, our thieves aren't inventive either. And,' the confident smirk he wore seemed like a permanent feature, 'the inspectors on our team are the best.'

Aileen snorted out a laugh. The police force at Loch Fuar was tiny. So tiny that you could count the number of officers in under five seconds. Callan was the only Detective Inspector.

THE FRENCH-TURNED-BRITISH COUPLE SNAGGED A BRUNCH of bacon, eggs and coffee from Aileen at about noon then disappeared back into their room promptly after.

Although Beaulieu had spoken a few words to her, his husband had all but forgotten Aileen existed. There were no polite compliments from him, nor were there any comments about the inn.

Neither of them let her know if the room was as per their needs. But Beaulieu was at least decent enough to thank her for the meal.

It was so odd, Aileen thought, her usual curiosity at the

forefront. As per their register entry, they were here from London. Most people travelled this far north to be away from their electronic gadgets and become one with nature, but the couple from the continent? They hadn't so much as asked for a brochure, just the Wi-Fi password.

Unusual indeed...

The sound of a rubber tyre skidding over a mud road broke Aileen's thoughts, and another car came to a halt in front of the inn.

A busy day indeed.

The Smiths had taken off as soon as they'd arrived, to explore. Martha was so exuberant she didn't seem like the sort to sit in a place for too long. She had dragged her husband along, though Aileen thought he looked knackered. He'd driven up from... Where was it? Edinburgh...

Aileen made a mental note to ask them to park in the lot when they returned. She'd barely gotten the chance to do so before.

Would they be back for a late lunch? Aileen bit her bottom lip.

It was a little nerve-racking: welcoming guests, seeing to their needs and maintaining an inn. What if she failed at this? What if they absolutely hated it and gave bad reviews? Bad publicity was the kiss of death for a business. She couldn't afford that.

No, Adventurous Aileen didn't worry; she didn't have any doubts. She breathed in confidence just as the handle on the wooden door rattled.

After a bit of a struggle, the person managed to get it open and a tall hefty man with hair as white as snow tumbled in. He looked like Santa Claus without the suit: his cheeks were pink, he had a long white beard, blue shining eyes and a well-fed belly.

'Oh! I ain't used to everything being on the wrong

side!' He thumped his large boots as he stepped inside. His accent didn't belong to Europe.

Another figure appeared beside him. She was tall as well but slender, a contrast to her husband.

This couple didn't need to introduce themselves; their accents told Aileen who they were. She had only one family booked from Canada: the Grants.

They'd been married for most of their lives, so their email had said. They were here to celebrate the coming of spring with their son and his wife.

'You must be the Grants.' Aileen grinned at their beaming faces.

The wife extended a lean, elegant hand. 'I'm Samantha, and this is my husband, Richard.'

Her voice was as elegant as her appearance, the mile-wide smile on her face the only thing that was Mrs Claus-like. She wasn't a grandmotherly sort of woman at all. In fact, she boasted glossy, well-styled brown hair. It was obvious she took great care of herself.

Richard smiled. 'I tend to forget my manners. This one does it for me.' He laughed at his wife and they shared a loving look.

'I'll get the bags,' he said and took off as Samantha completed the formalities.

When it was all done Aileen released a sigh. The Grants had settled in just fine.

They were ravenous so she cooked beans on toast for them. They wanted something 'breakfast like'.

They sat at the table asking Aileen questions about Scotland: kilts, Celtic traditions, the songs, the dance, whisky, haggis and everything else.

How typical!

They seemed the most normal and delightful couple. A perfect pair in Aileen's mind: the sophisticated wife and the forgetful husband. Their happy temperament and easy conversation came as a welcome change. At least they weren't snooty like Legrand.

As the afternoon waned off, the Grants excused themselves and went up to their room. Their son would be arriving the next day and staying for a week, while they would be staying for two.

That reassured Aileen that the older Grants had confidence in her inn. Reopening on the Friday of a long weekend had been an amazing idea.

Aileen was booked solid for the five rooms she'd renovated in the last few weeks. Even if the inn had a capacity for more people, starting small felt right. She could gain some experience this way.

The one thing she knew was business and the workings of one. And if all went to plan, her books would soon be in the black.

Aileen sneaked in a quick break in the early evening, then Isla dropped in to help make dinner. The middle-aged woman had become an unexpected best friend.

They gossiped a bit about the 'couple from the continent' as they'd agreed to name them. What did Legrand think of himself? What were they thinking travelling up here so ill-prepared? Who was Legrand? How was he so rich?

'Jeweller – that's what he wrote on the register,' Aileen whispered to Isla. She was sure gossiping about guests was a bad policy for any innkeeper but this was her first time. Who could she talk to beside Isla?

And the best part: Isla joined in, undeterred.

'Do you think he's into smuggling?' Isla was always looking for a scandal it seemed.

'What would they be doing here?'

'Loch Fuar is known to be secretive,' Isla said in a thick

accent. She did that when she became too excited, Aileen had quickly learnt. 'It's the perfect place to smuggle goods. No one looks at the wee Scottish towns.'

'Have you seen the series *Shetland*?' And so their talk continued.

When dinner was ready, Isla set the table. Much as she'd enjoy observing Aileen's guests, she had to leave; her family were waiting for her.

With nothing else to do, Aileen patiently waited for her guests to arrive, rubbing her hands together with excitement.

What happened when you mixed varied spices?

Maybe it wasn't a tradition at most inns but she wanted her first guests to know each other and mingle. In the hopes of getting them to socialise, she'd asked them to come for dinner at 7 p.m.

Aileen's nerves told her it seemed like a bad idea now.

Surprisingly, the Smiths were the first to turn up. Dave smiled weakly at Aileen. They were followed by the Canadian couple.

Legrand arrived alone.

At the archway leading up to the dining room, he cleared this throat then gave the entire room a sullen look.

An old vintage dining table, rickety chairs with pastel blue cushions and a fireplace behind the head chair clearly wasn't something he approved of.

'My husband shall be delayed,' he said in a cultured voice.

Richard Grant beamed at him. 'Are you from Belgium?'

'France,' came the curt and short reply.

'The country of cheese and wine,' Samantha Grant supplied.

'French fries are not French,' Richard tried to make a subtle joke.

Legrand regarded him with a look but stayed silent.

His husband panted as he walked briskly into the dining room. 'I apologise for the delay.' He didn't explain further.

'I like French fries – they're so crispy,' Martha Smith mumbled. She seemed rather down this evening, completely different from the enthusiastic woman who'd greeted Aileen earlier.

Legrand gave the table a cool look. 'The French have dignity and elegance. Subtlety too.'

That prim sentence had the potential to explode into an all-out battle.

'Hope you enjoy potatoes. We have a traditional Scottish dish called Clapshot this evening with mince.'

'What's a Clapshot?' Martha Smith asked, her voice reserved.

Aileen tried to sound as chirpy as she could. 'Clapshot is mashed tatties and neeps topped with butter. Tatties is what we call potatoes. My gran-'

'Potatoes with butter!' Legrand's tone was indignant. 'I want some food, Ms Mackinnon. Something healthy. Potatoes!' He threw the cream white napkin onto the plate. Loud stomping feet travelled up the stairs as he went up to the guest room.

A bit self-conscious, Aileen looked at her guests. Had it been a bad choice? She'd thought they'd appreciate it, and Isla and the lady at the grocery store had agreed with her. It wasn't as if she was serving them whole potatoes rolled in butter!

She snapped out of her doubt. Aileen wasn't embarrassed – she was miffed. She'd cooked, hadn't she? With all her love and care to greet them with classic Scottish fare, her Gran's favourite. The man could go to hell!

Richard cleared his throat. 'He was rather rude.'

'Please excuse my husband – he's, um, stressed lately, very stressed.' Beaulieu stood. 'I apologise, but I must go, um…' He sighed, hurrying up the stairs.

That left four people at the table now.

Morale ran low, on the precipice of rendering the entire meal dull. No one spoke but for a few mumbles to pass the plate and a quick thank you after.

The silence felt uneasy.

Aileen stayed quiet too, not in much of a mood for conversation.

'Good night.' Martha Smith stood unexpectedly and left the room.

Samantha turned a gaze towards Aileen. 'Could I help clean up?'

'I've got it, Mrs Grant. You must be tired,' Aileen replied, a small polite smile on her face.

As the clock chimed again, silence descended once more over Dachaigh. Aileen's guests took the hint.

'Well, I'm off.' Richard Grant patted his belly. 'Nice cooking.'

But Aileen heard him when he mumbled to himself, 'Such nasty company – ill-mannered fool.'

Dave Smith excused himself too and stepped out for some fresh air, even though twilight had unfurled into night.

As a full moon beamed its ghostly light on the darkened Highland scape, Aileen got her answer.

Do not mix such different spices together – they explode in the pan!

❄

CHAPTER FOUR

C allan Cameron woke up groaning and cursing. His muscles popped as he did his best to stretch. He clasped the aching right knee. That darn thing.

The pain was an unshakable reminder of victory over darkness, but it left a bitter taste in his mouth.

It was still very early—not even a stray ray of sunlight painted the glittering, star-strewn abyss overheard. Calm, it was his favourite time of day. With no one but him around…

Callan's shoulders protested, begging for some exercise.

A gruelling run was the best cure for the stiffness.

When the first nascent rays of the sun streaked from behind the mountains, Callan panted through a rocky trail. He knew it so well; he'd whizzed past these trees as a hopeful lad and pounded the ground as a cautious man.

A timid chirp snapped the thin shard of the peaceful morning—a songbird that would awaken the cold Highland scene.

Ending his run with the rhythm of birdsong made Callan feel as Zen as a Japanese garden. Who needed gyms and earphones to keep them entertained when the Highlands set a staggering stage?

He'd missed them, this, the years he'd spent away. Nowhere in the world could it be as beautiful as it was at home.

The fir trees, the rocky mountains and the expansive loch…

Callan came to a rapid halt.

That was unusual. With the sharp, unshakable eye of a detective inspector, he observed.

No one was ever around this early, especially here. But as the sky turned lighter, he could see two figures standing beside the cold loch. Neither were moving.

He peered closer as a bird rustled restlessly in its nest.

Were they male or female?

The figure facing the other was definitely male. Against the backdrop of the morning light, Callan could see him leaning towards the other person. He shook his hands in a stiff gesture with unhinged passion.

The other figure wore a baggy jacket and had a flurry of wild hair. The area around the loch was rocky, so judging the two of them based on their height was hopeless.

Abruptly the hand-shaking stopped, and instead, the man raised an accusatory finger at the other person. But the other person had turned to face the loch waters, apparently disinterested in whatever their companion had to say.

It was strange. Callan was sure none of the locals would be down there this early. They weren't foolish enough to arrive before sunlight had swept the landscape; too many men had died braving that road and the enigmatic loch's edge.

He looked the other way, towards Dachaigh, but the two figures were just too far away from the inn given they were still in the wee hours of the morning. And could a stranger drive down there using that deadly road, in the dark?

Callan shrugged. It wasn't illegal to stand by the loch, was it?

Unless something went wrong.

He squared his now limber shoulders. If it did, he'd step in to do what he'd always done: serve and protect.

His feet thudded on the mud road again as Callan took off running.

The two people by the loch never noticed him.

AILEEN HAD ADAPTED TO AN INNKEEPER'S LIFESTYLE - SHE woke with the sun and tried hard not to sleep on her feet.

It was time to cook breakfast. Breakfast was something that had been a luxury when she'd been toiling away at her demanding desk job. Back then, she'd be lucky to snag a steaming cup of coffee before braving the gruelling morning rush hour.

Her guests were sound asleep. Lucky them, Aileen huffed as she rubbed her droopy eyes. There was not a single stirring from any of their rooms.

She gathered all the produce, cleaned and dusted, all the while fighting off face-splitting yawns.

Isla came through the side door and into the kitchen. 'Hiya!'

'As long as you come bearing fresh bread, you're welcome.'

'As long as I get your scrumptious omelette, I have bread,' she sang back.

41

They both smiled at each other.

And with the next breath, Isla began her morning newscast. She told Aileen about her bairn, about the milkman who'd dropped in late, the chicken she'd cooked last night, and an impending meeting of the local business community.

When Aileen had left the city for this tiny town, scepticism had burned a nasty wedge in her heart. What if they treated her like an outsider? What if they hated her? But she had done something she hadn't managed all those years in the city: make a friend she was comfortable with.

The warmth and acceptance Isla offered was a treasure.

Together, just like the previous night, they cooked and set the table.

Isla, who'd never left the bakery in the wee hours, now felt no qualms about driving down to the inn instead. In exchange for her fresh bread, she got steaming hot gossip about Dachaigh's guests.

As Aileen narrated the dinner incident, Isla grinned, as though she'd never heard of a more interesting bunch.

'I dread them all assembling for breakfast now,' Aileen sighed.

'Why dread? It's as exciting as can be! Using your metaphorical spices, now you'll see what happens when you have a shimmering fire underneath. Wish I could be here!'

What could happen? Nobody could have guessed.

The Grants came in early. Richard Grant looked half asleep.

'This one wants to go bird watching!' He shot a half-annoyed, half-loving look at his wife.

She smiled. 'Yes! My friend told me it's something I must do.'

They chose a cup of coffee each. Richard picked up a few muffins. His wife decided on the healthy option: a bowl of fruit.

The clatter of china and cutlery rang out as the conversation ran dry – last night's dinner was a heavy elephant in the room.

Martha Smith pranced in, a spring in her step. She was smiling, but the smile didn't reach her eyes. In fact, Aileen observed, her eyes looked forlorn.

'Oh!' she gasped, hands covering the only feature of her face that held any glee. 'I... I...'

Finding nothing to say, she shrugged and walked towards the table.

'G'morning,' Samantha Grant greeted her with a courteous smile.

Martha merely bowed her head in acknowledgement.

The bright morning light didn't shine its cheer inside the dining room; it was all stiff and formal in there. Aileen hadn't a clue how to break the ice. It had frozen solid the night before.

Martha flashed a cordial smile at the Grants and looked over at Aileen. 'Dave'll be here soon.' She cleared her throat.

After the Grants left, the deafening silence stretched on. Martha sat by herself, chewing absentmindedly and staring off into space. Her face had fallen into a scowl.

A breeze picked up outside, but it didn't dare sway the dullness that descended over Dachaigh.

Wasn't it Dave's birthday weekend? That's what they'd told her. So why the long face?

Unlike the local people, Aileen knew the importance of privacy. She didn't pry.

Abruptly, Martha's chair screeched against the wooden floor. She pointed out a distracted hand. 'I'll be outside.'

The door clicked in place behind her.

What in the world was going on with the Smiths? They'd seemed like an ordinary couple. A couple out to celebrate the husband's birthday. Shouldn't they be spending the day together?

But what did Aileen know about couples? She couldn't remember the last time she'd gone down to the pub! Her love life had been flushed down the drain long ago.

The French duo never appeared for breakfast.

Perhaps her cooking was not the quality they were used to. She didn't give two hoots. Everyone loved her cooking, Aileen reassured herself with a definitive nod – if they didn't, something was wrong with their taste buds.

Yes, that was the new Aileen: strong and confident.

The chime attached to the front door tinkled and the latest bane of Aileen's existence stepped in. Detective Inspector Callan Cameron looked well-rested and prim in his all-black outfit.

'Isla says ye make a smashing cup of coffee.' Just to irk Aileen some more it seemed, Callan punctuated that with a challenging smirk, but what could she do?

She sat him down at the kitchen counter, a warm cup of coffee in his hand, then raised a questioning eyebrow. 'And the reason I find an inspector at my door this morning is?'

Callan paused as he took a sip of his coffee.

'Ye didn't have any qualms about me helping to repair this place. I was around a lot during that time.'

'I've guests now and it's breakfast hour. What'll they think about finding an officer of the law at their inn?'

'That the inn serves decent coffee.' This time Callan curled just the left side of his lips upward.

Aileen's retort died in her throat when the front door swung open and a woman strode in. She had curly dark blond hair enveloped around a small head. The short hair befitted her tiny face very well.

A compact woman of about middle age, she was dressed in heels and a suit, completely out of place in the rugged Highlands.

The last thing Aileen needed was a high-handed guest – a female version of Legrand.

A stomping of boots followed the elegant lady, and a pale man with a mop of bright red hair and a frown on his rumpled face emerged.

The woman gave him a disinterested look.

'We can't possibly be staying here.' He gestured at the reception area.

The elegant woman turned to him. 'Why ever not?' A completely unexpected grin split her face. 'Aunt Milly lived here when she came to Loch Fuar. She loved this place.'

When Aileen walked through to the reception area, the lady shone the full beam of her bright smile on her. 'Siobhan, that's what my Aunt Milly told me. The gentlest and best innkeeper she'd ever met. My aunt travelled a lot, from Asia to South America. She went to every continent except Antarctica!'

'Siobhan is my grandmother.' Aileen smiled cordially. 'Your aunt sounds like a daring woman.'

The woman nodded. 'You have large shoes to fill.' She seemed friendly enough. 'We are the Cooks,' she continued in a cultured voice.

Before Aileen could respond, Callan made an appearance. Aileen internally rolled her eyes. Hadn't she just told him about impressions?

With a smile, he introduced himself. Her new guests cast a suspicious glance at Aileen.

She quickly interrupted their thoughts. 'Inspector Cameron helped the local team renovate this place.'

'Aye,' he agreed, raising his cup. 'Enjoy yer stay here. Any worries, ye can find me at the station.'

Crude, that's what this man was.

'I'm John Cook.' The man seemed priggish.

'Susan Knight.' With a click of her heels she approached Aileen and raised a card. 'If you'd check us in please.'

By noon, Aileen patiently awaited the arrival of the younger Grant couple. They were the only guests left to make an appearance.

Ten guests. Aileen shook her head in exasperation. Six had already been a handful!

Despite her minimal people skills, she'd tried to start conversations, but apparently, her efforts weren't enough to fulfil her primary duty: keep your guests happy.

As if on cue, Legrand descended the stairs.

He looked around. Sensing no one nearby, he cast a superior gaze at Aileen. 'Anywhere nearby we might find a decent meal?'

Don't look down your long snooty nose at me, you—

Aileen could only dream of flinging those words at him. Instead, she cleared her throat of her mean thoughts, but before she could reply, the sound of a car door slamming shut interrupted her.

A man wearing a backpack jogged in. 'Dad's so right! It's like I'm in Outlander!'

He wore hiking clothes, with a pair of sturdy bulky boots. A camera swung by his side. Gaping, he admired the interiors of the inn.

'Hello.' The man waved at a displeased Legrand.

'*Mon Dieu!* The lowly company I'm subjected to.' Such unkind words should have been muttered privately but were just loud enough for the new guest and Aileen to hear.

Legrand turned 180 degrees and strode away.

'I'm sorry.' Aileen hastily apologised to the vibrant young man. 'Um, it's... It's...'

'A difficult guest – I understand. Mom was super excited when she called. Found some cool birds and such.' He spoke in a heavy accent, unlike his parents. 'Oh! I'm Jacob Grant. Please call me Jake though.'

Judging by his cherub-like face, he looked to be in his mid-twenties. A thick gold ring glistened on his finger.

'My wife's out clicking pictures. I hope I brought enough memory cards!' He laughed.

Susan Knight appeared in the doorway.

'Ms Aileen... Oh, I thought...'

'Hello.' Jake beamed at her. She grinned back.

Two happy people – could they flood this place with their delight?

'Oh, it's such a marvel!' Another happy human walked in. She headed straight for Jake and hugged him. 'Oh, it's the perfect place!' She looked moony-eyed.

After the dreary dinner of the previous evening, the three of her four new guests got along well. In fact, after checking in, the younger Grants and Susan Knight sat by the fireplace, sipping refreshing lemonade and chatting with each other.

They spoke about Scotland, its culture, and Loch Fuar.

Aileen left them to their own devices, playing the discreet hostess. Hopefully, their cheer would renew the air.

The older Grants didn't make an appearance till late in

the afternoon. They'd had a marvellous time bird-watching and trekking in the surrounding landscape.

Their son and his wife had retired to their room, so they too headed upstairs.

Martha Smith returned in the evening, looking flushed. Healthy colour stained her cheeks and her face held a small smile. She joyfully greeted Aileen and declined her offer for a snack.

Martha's husband was nowhere to be seen; he hadn't shown his face the entire day.

The Cook-Knights had had some soup and bread before diving into the inn's library. Aileen was glad she'd renewed the family area as a library. She loved to be surrounded by books, even if they weren't number-filled ledgers.

The middle-aged couple were each cosied up with a book. John had dozed off in the reclining chair, his book resting open on his chest, while Susan sat in one of the two high-backed chairs beside the fireplace. Next to her was the floor-to-ceiling wooden bookshelf. Apparently, the library was cosy enough for readers to lose themselves in, whether it was in the written word or their own dreamland.

As for Beaulieu and Legrand, after the latter's rude comment, they'd taken their car and headed towards town.

With nothing to do, Aileen busied herself in the kitchen.

Just then the back door clicked open.

'Your snotty guests made an appearance at Barbara's Tea Room. She handled them like a school headmistress.'

Here was Aileen's gossip radio, extra hand and entertainer all mixed into one.

Chattering, Isla rolled up her sleeves – she had a lot to narrate.

Steaming pots of savoury food effused mouth-watering aromas that drifted through the kitchen into the dining room.

What would happen during dinner? Aileen was a bit sceptical but excited. Last night's dinner had involved six reserved people, but today she had to add three jolly guests to the list.

THE DINNER HOUR CHIMED IN BY THE SOUND OF A CUCKOO. Aileen had bought the cuckoo clock home from the German Black Forest.

Martha Smith swooped down the stairs. She looked put together in her skirt and blouse and smiled at Aileen. 'It smells delicious. You're rather good at cooking.'

'Thank you.'

'Did your grandmother teach you? Talk in town is she was the best innkeeper you could ask for.'

'Aye, my grandmother is a dear. She brought love and life to this inn. It was like a child to her.'

'You have her skills,' she complimented. 'I wouldn't know where to start!'

Jake and Anne Grant giggled in, holding hands like newly-weds. Their infectious happiness seemed to raise Martha's mood and they began sharing details of their day – her walk alongside the stream and their interest in visiting Loch Fuar.

'They say it's dangerous to go down there,' Anne informed the small group.

'Dangerous yet fun!' Martha rubbed her hands together, leaning in.

'The road's winding and a little rough. So they say on the internet.' Anne whooshed out a breath.

'We could hire a car, babe,' Jake suggested. 'Driving on a difficult British road is hopeless.' He looked at Martha, 'You guys drive on the other side of the road and the other side of the car. It's like being toppled over.'

'Jacob!' Samantha Grant sauntered over to her son and the family embraced each other heartily. Ohs and ahs, with kisses and cheery shouts, puffed out affection into the air.

'Did you hear about the Rembrandt sketch pieces?' Richard said to his son. 'Apparently, they're conducting an auction soon.'

'Oh, you two! It's not time to talk shop,' Samantha chided.

John Cook entered the room. He gave a dispassionate glance at the dinner guests and then took a seat.

'What is it you do?' Martha asked the Grants as Aileen began serving the evening's meal: an aromatic shepherd's pie.

'There's pudding later.'

'You are a dear!' Richard announced jubilantly.

'We run an art gallery,' Samantha told Martha.

'How exciting!'

'Yeah, and we once had a…' With vivacious gestures, Samantha rambled on.

Except for John, everyone seemed engrossed in the lively conversation. He stared out of the window, looking into the night.

Aileen mused at the climate in her inn. It was very contrary to yesterday's nastiness: everyone was laughing!

'He didn't!'

The group broke into giggles and snorts.

'Yeah, he did! Sent us empty canvases, said he felt empty within. Not a scratch of paint on any of them. And when I—' Jake broke off as Dave Smith walked in, the British man's demeanour too serious for the company he stood amidst.

Martha smiled at her husband. He took a seat next to her and nodded at John.

After introductions, Samantha asked Dave, 'What about you? What do you do?'

'I'm a doctor.' He shook his hands vaguely. 'My wife's a homemaker and a talented designer.' He looked towards Martha with adoration.

A flushed Martha replied, 'Well, interior decorating magazines are such fun! I'm obsessed.'

Just like that, the conversation flowed once more and continued long after pudding was served. Everyone seemed to enjoy themselves – everyone except John Cook, who sat aloof and told no one where his wife was.

No, he looked out as if he knew bad could swallow the good in one swift gulp. And there was nothing good about this night.

CHAPTER FIVE

Martha announced she'd found an interesting book in the library. 'It's wonderful that you've got a library in the inn!'

Her husband declared he was retiring for the night. His eyes looked droopy; he'd been rubbing at them throughout the night, and his feet trudged heavily up the stairs.

Aileen had handed over the brochure for the local museum to Dave as he'd left. It had a free pass they could use the next day.

The Grants spoke for a while. They seemed like a close-knit family. Aileen gave them their privacy and locked up for the night.

She fastened all the larger windows, double-checking each lock, just in case. It was her upbringing, a product of living in the city: locking up was now a habit.

And double-checking was her self-doubt. Aileen huffed an exasperated sigh. No one changed overnight.

She reached into her pocket for the innkeeper's keys, fiddled a bit, felt around her trousers, then squished the pocket in her hands. Where were they?

Her heart thudded, growing louder with every beat. She never lost anything, not even when she was a child. Aileen was a person who always kept a thorough stock of her erasers, pencils and notes.

Where had she seen her keys last?

Hastily she walked into the kitchen, her heartbeat quickening until it burned in her chest.

She checked the service closet. Maybe she'd left them here when she fetched the mop?

Fiery flames of panic licked around her heart.

Where were her keys?

She jogged out into the drawing room. The Grants had retired to bed, leaving only the golden glow of the lamp to cover the room in a warm blanket of peace.

She turned down the lamps in the reception, leaving just enough light for Martha to make her way to bed later, and spun around to head up the stairs.

Something glinted on the reception counter and Aileen let out a sigh full of relief. There they were!

How irresponsible she had been! No one should have access to the keys apart from the innkeeper. That was rule number one. The keys should be on her at all times.

Hadn't her diligent grandmother taught her that?

At that thought, Aileen's face lit up in an affectionate smile. She'd best call her gran. It had been a while.

Despite the late hour, Aileen knew Siobhan would be awake. She loved those late-night horror shows.

Siobhan was a strange woman; sturdy and stubborn despite her age. She picked up on the third ring. 'You best have a reason to interrupt me,' came a strict but loving voice. It was as strong as she remembered, with not a shiver of old age evident.

'Gran.'

'Ah. Did you burn down ma inn?'

'No! I just called to ask how you were.'

'Fit as a fiddle I am. And ready to break the neck of anyone who disturbs Horror Nights!'

Aileen rolled her eyes. These were words of affection, reserved for her kin.

The best reply to that was a rebuke. 'Have you been naughty? Troubling dear Nancy?'

'The lass keeps pushing those horrid medicines down ma throat. Told her I'd rather a glass of whisky. Do me loads of good.'

It was common knowledge that her grandma had ways to sneak in whisky. She enjoyed a regular dose.

'Is everything fine, dearie?' Despite the hard exterior, Siobhan carried a soft heart underneath.

'Aye, everyone's been kind and helpful.'

'Small town wonders. Rory Macdonald tells me you're tight with Isla. Good lass as ever she is. Married the good-hearted Daniel.'

'She's wonderful.'

'She helped me out some before Daniel stole all her time. Heard she has a wee bairn.'

'Ah yes, little Carly!'

And so Aileen spent a good hour laughing and joking with her grandmother.

Even though she was away, Siobhan kept her ears to the ground when it came to Loch Fuar's gossip. She had her trusted sources. And Aileen realised, she'd pumped her granddaughter for information as well – not about the town per se, but about the frustrating Detective Inspector Callan Cameron.

As Aileen readied herself for bed, Martha Smith read her novel. She was lost in a bygone era. A time when turbaned traders crossed great distances on horseback, pounding down the miles under the sweltering sun. Would they find the key to save their ailing prince?

The inn fell silent around Martha, but she never noticed the eerie quiet.

As Aileen leaned back against her headboard, she let out a groan. It had been a long day. And tomorrow she had to be up early again. Being an innkeeper was demanding! A yawn escaped her lips.

She was reaching over to flick off the bedside lamp when she heard it: a muffled patter of footsteps. The thudding of Aileen's heart seemed louder than the rhythmic steps. She inhaled a lung full of breath and froze in place. That didn't mean her heart stopped. Leaning over, Aileen cursed when her bed creaked.

The sound of crickets enveloped Dachaigh again. And then she remembered. It would just be Martha, coming to bed. She was being silly.

With the click of the lamp's button, blackness swallowed the golden orb of light and Aileen settled down to sleep with a grin on her face. Her first day with ten guests had been a success. And it felt nice, talking to her grandmother; sleeping in the same bed Siobhan had slept in all those decades ago, the sheets tucked around Aileen's slumbering body with love.

Being here was like being with her grandmother. Siobhan had sounded happy on the phone call. That was good. Maybe it was time to pay a visit to the nursing home. She'd—

Aileen jerked up. What was that noise?

It sounded like a door being firmly clicked shut.

Aileen held her breath, her heart palpitating beyond control. If only it would be quiet!

She'd made a mistake leaving her keys out for everyone to see. There could be a burglar in the house!

For a few minutes, nothing stirred. Had the temperature dropped? The inn had turned as silent as a cemetery.

Shaking her head, Aileen cast this episode as a figment of her imagination. Hadn't she always had a wild one?

Cuddling into her pillows, Aileen pulled the covers up to her chin, snuggled in and was out like a light before anyone could warn her otherwise.

AILEEN FELT GROGGY AS SHE SHOWERED AND DRESSED FOR the day. Her disorientation had turned to lingering annoyance.

As she made her rounds and found everything as she'd left it the previous night, Aileen chided herself for her self-doubt. Uncertainty about herself was a feeling the new Aileen didn't entertain.

Pleased that everything was in place, she walked past the library. There, in a high-backed chair, was Martha Smith. She seemed to have dozed off; the book slumped on the floor beside her.

She fitted in the chair perfectly, and the room was still warm and cosy.

Aileen's irritation eased at finding her guest comfortable.

Isla bounced in late. Dark circles under her eyes made her look ghostly pale.

'Bairns are good to look at, but incredibly frustrating

otherwise! Did Carly sleep a wink last night? No!' Isla whisper yelled, gesturing vividly with her hands. 'That means we stay awake with her too. Crying her eyes out! Why? The Lord knows. And now, that little devil's asleep with a thumb tucked in her mouth—'

'And you look like a haunted woman,' Aileen finished.

'Aye!' Isla said indignantly. 'You could make me feel alive again with yesterday's dinner news.'

A sly smirk accompanied the demand.

Aileen huffed out a breath and protested that as innkeeper she couldn't gossip about her guests. But like Siobhan, Isla had perfected the art of milking gossip from everyone she met, whether they were a willing or unwilling participant.

Isla made a tsk sound. 'That's plain. Boring! I wish they'd be nasty to each other. It's more fun that way.'

'I wish not.' Aileen shot a pointed look at her friend. She was a fiend for a scandal.

Beaulieu and his husband were the first to make an appearance. The stubby Frenchman was in high spirits, though Louis Legrand was his usual sullen self.

It would be such a bore being married to a stiff man like him, Aileen thought. Her irritation piqued. They seemed to be fine as they took their seats.

Boisterous laughs announced the Grants' arrival before they stepped in. Legrand gave them the customary look down his pointed nose, while John Cook came down the stairs behind them, looking miffed.

Martha appeared then. 'Oh! I dozed off in the library all night.' Her giggles ended on a moan as she massaged her shoulders.

Richard Grant laughed with her. 'Hope you don't have a stiff neck!'

Susan Knight strutted in last. She looked elegant but

had replaced her suit and heels for trousers, a T-shirt and hiking boots.

'Where's Dave?' Martha looked around the table with a confused frown.

'He hasn't come for breakfast yet.' Aileen placed a plate piled high with food on the table.

Mouth-watering smells of coffee, eggs and toast wafted through the dining room.

'Oh, that's strange! We're supposed to go down to the museum today.'

'It's an exciting place.' Samantha Grant slapped her hands in enthusiasm.

Susan leaned in. 'They say on the internet that Loch Fuar has a history that goes back to the Celts.'

Martha muttered, 'I think I should go up and check. He never sleeps in.'

She strutted over to the staircase and hiked up quickly. They could hear her footsteps echoing along the floorboards as she walked to her room.

There wasn't another sound apart from the chirp of the birds outside and the occasional rattling of pots as Aileen continued to plate up breakfast.

Heavy clouds marred the grey sky, the brightness missing from the colours of spring.

The door upstairs creaked open as Martha pushed it – and then let out a blood-curling scream.

Such a horrendous sound!

It echoed through the inn and out around the mournful landscape of Loch Fuar.

CHAPTER SIX

The entire inn had bustled in a flurry of activity.

Perhaps a few of her guests had frozen at the plain horror of that scream, but the formerly prim and proper Aileen had somehow known.

Looking back, she'd always had a very keen intuitive sense. And her intuition had been ringing an alarm in her head ever since Martha Smith had enquired after her husband.

Maybe it was because of the preparedness that intuition brought, or perhaps it was her quick reflexes, but Aileen was flying up the stairs before Martha had hit the floor.

It was a terrifying scream, more sinister than a wolf's howl.

The door to the bedroom was pushed wide open, and in the doorway lay the prone figure of Martha Smith. She'd crumpled, unconscious to the floor.

Heavy footsteps echoed behind Aileen. Whoever it was would take care of Martha, she told herself. As the innkeeper, she had to find out what had happened to Martha's husband.

Nobody could have prepared themselves for the devastation she found inside the room. Blood drenched the entire bedspread, as crimson as a rose. And Lord, the smell! Not just the dried blood, but a gruesome, gut-burning stench Aileen could only document as the culmination of a life.

There could be no mistake.

Since – especially since… Aileen swallowed but immediately gagged – right in the centre of the bed, an elaborately hilted knife protruding from his chest, lay Mr Dave Smith… And yes, he was dead – as stone-cold as the early Neolithic men.

Detective Inspector Callan Cameron was enjoying his second cup of espresso when the call came.

He hadn't thought the neat and put-together Aileen Mackinnon could sound so shaken. She hadn't been hysterical, but she had made little sense. He'd only caught the words 'dead… Murder… Come quickly'.

Callan rubbed his scruff. His pace was a little languid as he headed to his car. It was true Loch Fuar hadn't seen a murder in decades, and he hadn't witnessed a murder in the town himself, but death, assassinations and killings – he had seen plenty of that circus in his career; sometimes much more than he could stomach.

But now wasn't the time to go back there, and Callan sealed those disturbing thoughts in the past – where they belonged.

Somebody had died.

With a frown, Callan reminded himself that he was now a detective inspector. And he would do whatever it took to achieve justice.

Callan's worn truck bobbled over the tiny bridge and swooshed down the rugged road. Unlike his laid-back demeanour, he drove with vigour.

Dachaigh emerged from behind tall trees.

From the outside, everything seemed calm. The heavy clouds had parted, the sun was now shining down on the old stone walls, while the flowers in the yard bloomed with cheerful colours and the blue windows added a touch of pleasantness to the entire scene.

The scene of a possible murder.

His heavy boots struck the gravelled pathway leading up to Dachaigh.

Dachaigh – home in English, he mused. Murder had come home.

The front door burst open to show a harried Aileen. Her usually neat locks now stuck out in weird angles, as if she'd pulled on them repeatedly. For the few weeks he'd known her, he'd never seen a single hair out of place on that pretty face. But now her eyes looked a little too wide, a little too bright.

'I've assembled everyone in the library. We got Martha Smith back to consciousness and I... I...' She spread her hands wide as if words had failed her.

'Where is it?' Callan nudged in a calm voice. Not everyone dealt with death steadily. It would have been strange if Aileen wasn't flustered, given the circumstances.

He came to a stop outside the room.

Death had come here with violence. Perhaps a controlled rage, but aggressive nonetheless.

Air played through the room. It was strange. Last night

had been a cold one; it seemed unlikely Dave would have left the window open. And Aileen had promised she'd let no one contaminate the scene.

The net curtains danced in the breeze, scooping the stench out of the room, while an additional thick pair of curtains by the window frames pulled on their restraints.

The sunlight set the cream net ablaze. It wasn't a dim room, and that made the blood gleam brighter.

The smell Callan could've recognised from a mile away. It was as intense as the picture before him.

Taking as much precaution as he could, he assessed the scene, scratching down notes in his pocket-sized diary before making a few phone calls.

Aileen gingerly walked up to the door, looking everywhere but inside the room.

'Um, they're all asking…' She squared her shoulders and started again. 'What can you tell us?'

'Ye can tell me. What do ye know about this man?'

Aileen told Callan his name, that he was here with his wife and according to the information they'd provided, he was a doctor.

'Oh, oh no! It was his birthday weekend.'

She shuddered out a breath, then rubbed her eyes. 'What can I do? His wife is distraught.'

'That's natural,' Callan sighed. Rudeness didn't help everyone. 'I've spoken with Rory Macdonald, my superior officer. And I've arranged for a team from the neighbouring town to assist. We don't have one in Loch Fuar to run tests. I'll be the primary on this investigation.'

Aileen nodded.

'I'd like to speak with yer guests, see yer security tape and then I must speak with ye too.'

'Right.' Aileen spread her hands. 'I've seen crime movies, but I'm not a fan.'

'Movies and reality are worlds apart.' He flashed his teeth, then turned serious once more. 'Walk me through yesterday.'

Aileen rubbed her hands over her arms. 'Could we talk in my chambers upstairs?'

The innkeeper's chambers were half the attic. Considering Callan's tall build, he felt like a giant walking into a dollhouse. The ceiling tapered dangerously low, almost brushing his hair.

When Aileen had first entered the tiny room, Callan thought it might've been a former closet – the cramped kind. Books were randomly scattered about, old and new, along with cardboard boxes and used-up tape. And the 'work desk' was an old table with sticks for legs. Who knew the innkeeper wasn't the disciplined type when it came to her belongings?

A small smirk played on Callan's face as he stuck his hands in his pockets, crossed his legs and leaned on the doorframe. Aileen sat down in the only chair.

It was silent in here, except for the constant sound of Aileen's feet tapping on the floor. She occasionally ran her fingers through her hair. A nervous habit, Callan mused.

'Yesterday,' he prompted.

She ran him through the day. How she'd cleaned up, cooked and welcomed four new guests. How Martha had eaten her breakfast alone and how she hadn't seen Dave Smith during the day.

'He came down for dinner, rather late. And he looked tired – said as much after dinner. He didn't speak much except for answering the occasional question.'

'And his wife? Where did she spend the night?'

'Oh, she was engrossed with a book in the library. I found her there this morning, fast asleep.'

Callan nodded as he wrote it all down. Then Aileen clamped her hands together.

'And during dinner, they were discussing plans to go down to the local museum today.'

Rough scrawling sounds echoed through Aileen's tiny study.

'Who found him?'

'Martha Smith. I went up when she screamed. I saw – I saw—' Aileen blubbered.

She looked embarrassed as she tucked her chin, staring at the floor. The scene had been a horrific one for the uninitiated…

Aileen dried her tears as quickly as they'd sprung up. 'I'm sorry, it's just – just… Sorry.' She looked everywhere but into Callan's concerned gaze. 'I'll get the others ready – you can interview them in the kitchen if you like.'

And with that, the cultured Aileen was back. She still looked distraught, but more than able to handle herself. She seemed to have a lot of strength in that tiny stature of hers – just like her formidable grandmother.

LIBRARIES HAD DONE NOTHING FOR CALLAN. HE'D ALWAYS found them the most boring place in the entire world, after supermarkets, where you ran into all sorts of unwanted company.

Although at Dachaigh, it was a different matter entirely. He looked at the group assembled here. One of them was, perhaps, a murderer.

As per the descriptions Aileen had provided, the red-haired woman who slumped in the high-backed chair, staring at her feet, was Martha Smith, the new widow. She wasn't crying though. That fact could work in his favour; nothing more convenient than a coherent spouse.

A short yet elegantly dressed man stood beside her, his hand on her shoulder: Jean Beaulieu. His husband – the snooty git, as Aileen had put it – stared out into the stunning Highland scenery.

An older woman and a young lass in her twenties sat holding hands, sniffing back tears: Samantha and Anne Grant. Their respective husbands loomed over them as if offering their protection.

An elegant lady, her hair and her clothes still neatly wrapped around her, stared at the books that ran from the floor to the tall ceiling: Susan Knight. John Cook stood with his legs crossed at the ankle, leaning on the bookshelves, hands in his pockets, staring at the carpeted floor.

An interesting mix of people, not just in nationalities but in style and age. Aileen walked in behind him.

Ten suspects.

It was time to reignite his interview skills.

Callan asked Louis Legrand to come in first. He seemed the most disinterested of the lot – something that intrigued Callan.

'What were ye up to last night?'

'What most people are, Inspector. Sleeping. I went to bed at ten.' He waved his hands in a vague gesture. 'Didn't go down for that meal Ms Mackinnon calls dinner.' He snapped out 'meal' as if it was something poisonous.

'Did ye hear anything before or after ye went to bed?'

He raised his chin. 'Not a word, nor any sound. It was quiet. I expect it to be. That's the least that lady can do.'

'If ye don't like it here, why stay?'

'It's the only place to stay. No wonder you have no tourism here. And I've paid the full price. I expect to make the most of it.' His attitude turned indignant.

Legrand knew more than he was letting on. Callan was excellent at reading people, especially consummate liars.

But he let this one go.

Next came Jean Beaulieu, his husband.

'Nasty business, n'est ce pas?' He plopped down on the high chair by the kitchen counter. 'Poor Mrs Smith is so broken.' He stared down at the counter.

'What happened this morning?'

'We came for breakfast — we'd skipped dinner. We weren't hungry last night. Mrs Smith asked where her husband was.'

Beaulieu looked up at Callan then. 'She'd spent the night in the library. So everyone said. Louis and I weren't there to see — as I told you, we didn't come down for dinner.'

'Had you met Dave Smith before?'

'Non...' With that he trailed off, emotion crowding behind his eyes.

Callan dismissed him. Unlike his stiff husband, Jean Beaulieu had had a genuine emotion in his posture and speech. He cared, but Callan could sniff it: the pretence under it all.

It had become almost methodical: one guest followed the other.

Susan Knight came next. She'd slept peacefully last night. She had been 'out like a light' as soon as her head had hit the pillow, so she said.

John Cook had been by her side. She'd retired to bed, tired after their long journey.

Apart from their brief conversation at the dinner table, she hadn't met Dave Smith before.

'I wish I could be of more help. He seemed like a man who adored his wife.' She looked out of the window behind Callan.

The day had turned out to be as pleasant as the morning: birds sang the tunes of spring, verdant trees swayed in the light breeze, and in the distance, Loch Fuar shone like a mirror beneath the cerulean sky.

Why would this incredible landscape have invited a killer into its midst?

John strutted in after his wife. 'Slept like a baby all night,' he said before sitting on the chair.

'Let me guess,' Callan said. 'Heard nothing, woke this morning and came for breakfast. Martha Smith screamed and ye ran.'

John raised one finger and shook it. 'No, I didn't run.' He gestured with his right hand. 'Everyone else dashed upstairs like it was a timed game. It was that man's birthday or something. Could've just been a surprise for his wife.' He snorted. 'Yup, surprised his wife alright.'

'The way a person screams in surprise and shock are very different, Mr Cook.'

John shrugged. 'I was beside Susie the whole night.'

'She can't testify to that.'

John's eyes lit up with barely contained fury. 'She was next to me the *entire* night. And she knows that,' he said through clenched teeth.

That was an unusual reaction.

But the person who followed next seemed even more outlandish to Callan. Richard Grant came in looking a little lost. He looked everywhere but at the inspector and sat with his shoulders slumped.

'Never seen such devastation. I've seen death though. Lost my mother right in front of my—' He broke off.

'What happened this morning? Could ye elaborate?'

'That young lady, Martha Smith, went upstairs to check up on her husband. Dave?' he questioned. 'And then – then...' Richard expelled a shivering breath. 'She screamed the place down. I went up. I think – I think the innkeeper went up first, like a bullet.'

He looked at his fingers; he'd placed on his lap.

'I saw him over her shoulder. Barely caught a glance before all hell broke loose. And then I – I caught Sam before she saw it all. Led the women downstairs and um... Um... Jake, he helped Beaulieu carry Martha downstairs. We got her to wake up.' He spread his hands. 'It's all a blur.'

Under all that distress was something else, something Richard wasn't saying.

Samantha Grant repeated more or less the same thing. She hadn't seen the mess. But her maternal instincts made her sob. 'I never... I never imagined...' She was visibly upset. In fact, she was the first of the lot he'd interrogated all morning who struggled to string words together.

'Did ye see Mr Smith?'

A sob and a shake of her head: no.

'Did ye hear anything strange last night, between dinner and breakfast?'

A sniff and another shake of her head.

All the while, her gaze was fixed somewhere near her feet.

With nothing more to add, Callan let her go.

Aileen and Jake Grant helped her out before Jake hustled back in.

'She's pretty shaken. We were just here for a holiday; to spend some time with each other. She's wanted to come here ever since I was a kid.'

He stood by the kitchen chair, looking straight at Callan.

Interesting, Callan thought. 'Could ye tell me what happened this morning?'

'Anne and I woke up. We enjoyed the incredible view from our room for a while, and then came down the stairs, where I must say, everything looked fine.'

He took a breath. 'Then my parents joined us and we sat down with everyone. I like this idea – having meals together. You get to meet so many people! And then, well, sanity went out the door.'

'Could ye elaborate what ye mean by "sanity went out the door"?'

'The woman screamed bloody murder – and so it was in this case! Dad ran up and, um, I followed. Come to think of it, the Cook guy didn't move a muscle. He turned to his wife instead.'

'And then what did he do?'

'Looked at her with some confusion? Frustration? Can't say.'

'Okay, so ye went up the stairs. Then what did ye do?' Callan guided the interview.

'I could see Dad turn pale and knew something was wrong. The innkeeper, yes she went up before any of us could react, like she knew something terrible had happened. She looked shell-shocked. And the woman, the dead man's wife, had collapsed onto the floor.'

He took another breath and looked out of the window, emotion now visible on his face.

'Dad took the other women – Susan, Mom and Anne – down. And the French guy, Beaulieu, had come up the

69

stairs too. He helped me carry Martha out. But – but when I went to help Ms Mackinnon pick her up off the floor, I saw…'

'Alright, please send Anne Grant in… Yer wife?' Callan raised a questioning eyebrow at Jake.

'Yes, we've been married for about a year… Married young.' He gave a half-hearted laugh.

Anne Grant was a young woman in her early twenties. She constantly worried the hem of her navy jacket. She had straight blond hair mixed with some blue streaks.

'I just – I just…' She looked around her. 'I've never had another human being die in the same house as me. And – and..' She sniffed into her white handkerchief.

On it, embossed, were the letters JG – her husband's handkerchief. How odd, Callan thought. Who embossed their handkerchief these days?

'Did ye see Dave Smith this morning?' Callan asked.

She shook her head, still sniffing. 'They all said he was dead in his own blood. And it was his birthday this weekend.'

She blew her nose loudly.

'What happened when ye went up there?'

'We ran up, and then Richard, my father-in-law, came towards Samantha and I. Told us it was best we went back down. But from the look on everyone's faces and the unconscious woman on the floor, I knew it was something horrible.'

Callan nodded as he recorded their conversation. 'And who did you see when Richard led ye down the stairs?'

Anne took a deep breath. 'I don't remember.'

'Tell me whatever ye recall.'

'The Frenchman. Not the uptight one – Jean Beaulieu? He came up behind me. I heard him talking to Jake. Jake!

He was dragging the unconscious woman out of the doorway.'

'What did Jake do then?'

'He dragged her some way, then I think Beaulieu helped him carry her down the stairs.'

'And who tried to walk up the stairs as ye descended?'

'John Cook.'

'And Mr Legrand?'

'I didn't see him anywhere.'

CHAPTER SEVEN

The only way for Aileen to stay busy was to cook. Callan had informed her that more police were on their way, and an hour and a half after he'd arrived, a forensic team followed.

She'd shown them the way. The other police constable, Robert Davis, had officially warned all her guests to stay in the town of Loch Fuar.

Even now her lodgers were scattered in the library or the drawing room.

Martha Smith was still distraught. The paramedic had checked up on her and advised rest in another empty room a while ago.

Aileen had squeezed two jugfuls of lemonade – for guests as well as the investigative team.

It was such a horrid affair, murder. And it was especially disastrous for her fledgling business.

Hadn't she wanted adventure? Well, she had it now. Aileen thought sarcastically.

What would she tell her grandmother? Murder! In Dachaigh. At her home.

Aileen worried her lip. No, she told herself, she couldn't let panic take over now. She locked it away with her self-doubt.

Callan Cameron walked in. 'Fascinating,' he muttered. 'She cooks as well.'

Hadn't he already eaten food she'd cooked? The inspector wasn't quite right in the head. And he walked funny too.

Aileen shook herself. Rambling, even in her head, was a nervous tell.

Callan winced. Clearing his throat he got straight back to business. 'As soon as the doctor allows, I'll be here to ask Martha Smith some questions.'

Aileen nodded. 'What have you found out?'

'That a man who called himself Dave Smith has been murdered.'

'I got that from the scene I witnessed a couple of hours ago,' Aileen retorted.

Callan snorted out a laugh. 'Can't tell ye.'

'But – but I need to know!' Aileen stuttered, a bit of hysteria finding a way out of her Pandora's box.

Callan pointed a finger at her. 'What you need to do is stay put. No one leaves town: not ye nor yer guests. And I shall be investigating.' He pointed to himself.

'And,' he added, 'maybe look into getting some more security cameras!'

Aileen huffed out a breath. 'I never thought I'd need them! And guests need privacy.'

Shaking his head, Callan looked at the ceiling as if offering up a prayer. 'Installing cameras in the corridors is not an invasion of privacy.'

'Aren't you the one who told me thieves in Loch Fuar are all dum-dums?'

Callan rolled his eyes and walked out of Dachaigh, into the dreary afternoon.

Aileen had installed security cameras at two spots: above the front and back doors. Wouldn't the killer be caught on camera trying to sneak in?

No one could have entered or exited after she'd locked the doors. So the murderer would have had to break in to enter. But there had been no signs of splintered glass or locks… That meant it was a guest who'd committed murder or…

It took Aileen a few minutes to process it all. She was a suspect too! Being adventurous was one thing; being looked at for murder was something else – something far more dangerous!

She jogged out into the reception area, fumbled into her coat and ran outside.

Callan stood talking to a member of the forensic team. The woman turned as Aileen approached, nodded at her and went back inside.

'Aye, Ms Mackinnon?'

'I forgot to tell you, I heard noises last night.'

'Is that so?' Was he mocking her?

Aileen imagined punching Callan in the gut. She was just being honest to the police, as the law dictated!

'Footsteps, and a door closing. I think. I thought it might've been Martha at the time, or that I'd imagined it, but now I'm sure it was someone moving about.'

Callan folded his arms over his chest, looking sceptical. 'And what time was this?'

Aileen looked at him, mildly annoyed. 'I spoke to my gran last night. We spoke well up to midnight. I went to bed around fifteen minutes after. I heard footsteps and a door being shut. I waited for a while to see if I could hear anything else but it was silent.'

'I'll keep that in mind,' Callan said, before turning towards his car.

Aileen shrugged frustrated. He wouldn't listen to her, would he? Typical Callan Cameron!

It looked like she'd have to do some digging herself. What if he wasn't good at his job and something terrible occurred? Like he pointed the blame on her... Or worse, never caught the actual killer.

Her inn would be doomed from the get-go.

THE FORENSIC TEAM DID WHAT THEY ALWAYS DID AT A murder scene, and people swarmed in and out of Dachaigh well into the late afternoon.

All of Aileen's guests remained indoors, the Grants and Jean Beaulieu trying to console a heartbroken Martha.

Knowing that she was the last person who could help console others, Aileen took to cooking high tea instead.

Isla bustled in, full of worry but supportive and with a patient ear.

'You know, I could help you,' she said, once Aileen had revealed her plans to investigate. She wanted to stand by her friend. Even if that meant hunting a murderer. Besides, scandalous affairs were hard to come by when you were happily married and had a toddler at home, so Isla informed her.

'I know you would, Isla. And thank you for that. But I have no clue where to begin.'

Isla thought for a moment. 'You know who Callan would divulge secrets to?'

'Who?'

'The one person who has control over his morning coffee.'

Aileen raised her eyebrows. 'You can't threaten a police officer! Besides, he's a tough nut to crack.'

'Police officer? Threaten? Why I shall do no such thing!' Isla waved her hands. 'But you're right about the other thing: he is a tough nut.'

Silence descended except for the sounds of movement and scraps of conversation drifting from upstairs. The people walking up and down her stairs in the background were just a harsh reminder of what had transpired.

All because of a murder…

Is this how it felt, to have a murderer in your midst?

She'd read thrillers and felt uneasy, but the reality was different. Her emotions ranged from fear to anxiety to excitement, sometimes all at the same time! Adrenaline spiced up the cocktail and wired her brain to work furiously at the problem.

As if struck by lightning, Aileen snapped her fingers. 'I know! We need to look into the supporting documents.'

'What do you mean?'

'Let's do some digging into my guests' personal lives.'

Isla smiled devilishly. 'Now that idea I like.'

Solving a murder was more interesting to Isla than running her bakery. She'd called Daniel and asked him to look after the wee one. When he'd guessed something was cooking, he'd asked his wife what she was up to.

'I ken ye; I ken that glee in yer voice – you're scheming or plotting.'

'Daniel! I don't scheme; I merely help.'

'Right ye do,' came Daniel's sarcastic reply.

Aileen smiled at the side of the exchange she could hear. Apparently, Daniel knew his spouse too well but he let it go.

Isla had a small smile on her face as she clicked off. 'I

have resources – gossip ones. I can tap those; you can use the tech.'

With that Aileen found herself studying the register.

As per policy, she had checked the passports of all the Grants and both of the Frenchmen. Their ID had seemed genuine. Could one of them have lied?

A murder needed planning, and surely it would be easy for someone who'd commit murder to forge their ID.

Her suspicion landed first on Louis Legrand. He was just snooty enough to think no one could hold him accountable for murder. And where had all his wealth come from?

But what motive could he have had?

Aileen shook her head and looked back at the register. Dave Smith had been a doctor, so he'd claimed, and her gaze moved to the near-illegible entry he'd made in the register. He wrote like a doctor alright. She strained her eyes to decipher what he'd scrawled there. He'd come down from Edinburgh – that much she understood.

It had been foolhardy not to ask the rest of her guests for their IDs. They'd had booking numbers from Dachaigh's website. How could that number have been sufficient?

The only information she'd collected were their names, the number of people who'd be staying with them, the days they'd be staying and the payment information – which for the most part was in cash.

With a frustrated frown, Aileen hunched over her laptop. She knew how to dig and find information where there was none available.

In the search bar, she typed in 'Dr Dave Smith'.

There were many across the country, so she narrowed the search to Edinburgh. That brought the search results down to a manageable number.

Now all she had to do was find out which one of them was the murdered man.

A FEW MINUTES AWAY, DETECTIVE INSPECTOR CALLAN Cameron sat in his uncomfortably small chair. He clutched his right leg, massaged it for a while and sighed. It had been a while since he'd seen murder or smelled brutal death.

Callan drummed his fingers on the arm of the chair. Eleven people inside the inn and no one had gone in or out, according to the security cameras. The rest of the windows had been fastened shut, and none were broken. If someone had climbed up to the first storey, they'd leave footprints on the windowsill, and there were none.

And who would murder a tourist? Smith hadn't ever been to Loch Fuar, nor had any altercation with anyone in the couple of days he'd been here.

No, the murderer had to be one of the eleven people inside the inn.

The rapping of a knuckle on glass broke the silence. It was his superior officer.

'I'm leaving. Let me know where you get with the investigation.' And with that, the elderly Rory Macdonald, the head of a three-member police force, clomped off.

The investigation had fallen to Callan as he had experience. He'd also been first on the scene.

Callan set up his incident board, the first since… Well, since a while.

He liked to get his chronology right. Flipping through the reports, Callan assessed what the forensic team had told him so far. The medical examiner had gauged the time of death to be around early morning. Aileen had said she'd heard footsteps at about midnight. No, that didn't get down with the TOD. Still, Callan made a note of it. No other person inside the inn had heard anything.

He scratched the prickly scruff that had grown on his chin.

The medical examiner's report should come in soon, so he hoped.

His chair protested as he plopped back into it with some force and shut his eyes.

He brought the scene into focus.

Everyone had always complimented him on his photographic memory. So now he thought back, his nose scrunched up as it tinkled with the awful smell of blood. Callan remembered how the curtains looked and the body – prone and lifeless.

The bed had been queen-sized, a little rumpled by a man in sleep. Dave Smith had been in the exact centre of the bed, spread-eagled. He'd worn striped pastel-green pyjamas and was barefooted, his body cold and stiff.

The T-shirt of the pyjama had been in place – no buttons were broken or undone as far as Callan could recall. The bedside lamp had stood just where it ought to be, and even the deceased doctor's spectacles lay untouched.

A man who'd been stabbed would put up a fight. But nothing looked disturbed, not even the bedspread. Perhaps he'd been incapacitated first.

Callan shuffled his legs, then lifted them over his desk in a relaxed gesture. He rested a hand on his chin, eyes still firmly shut.

He brought the pliant corpse into focus— Caucasian, dark brown hair, slightly on the heavier side and just over six feet. The dead man would never see the bright sun nor feel the breeze that played with his eyelashes.

What had killed him? And who?

The murder weapon – Callan could see that. That was the real eye-catcher. A long blade, the kind which usually had a scabbard. And its hilt, that was the interesting bit: a glowing jade green, well-polished and shiny, the design of a Celtic symbol etched upon it in gold.

Was the symbol significant? Callan did not know Celtic symbols. He'd only seen them in old church ruins.

The blade that came with the elegant hilt was sinister: as sharp as shark's teeth. Callan knew how it would have felt in the hands of the killer, like a knife scooping up soft butter.

He shook his head. *Focus on the scene,* he told himself.

All guests had kept their windows shut – at least that's what his external analysis of the inn had told him. Everyone except Dave Smith. He'd worn light pyjamas, but the temperature had dropped to single digits that night. Why open the window?

The killer could have opened it perhaps. They'd found no fingerprints though. And the window could only be opened from the inside – one of the meagre security features Aileen Mackinnon had installed. This proved the killer had to be one of the eleven people who had spent the night at Dachaigh.

And yes this was premeditated murder.

Callan opened his eyes; they shone brightly. He hurriedly penned down his notes.

Next, he scrutinised the wife. She'd been asleep in the library, all alone with no one to alibi her, but she'd been distraught and surprised when she found her husband, just as an unexpectedly widowed wife would be. Or was it just good acting? Callan scratched his beard again. Something about Martha Smith smelled foul; something wasn't quite right.

As alibis went, how did the others stand? They'd all gone to sleep – so deeply in fact that no one had heard a thing.

Callan smiled a devilish smile. An inn full of eleven people, and everyone except for the innkeeper slept like a baby... Humbug!

He rose to his feet and began pacing when the front door of the small police station opened. He stepped out of his office and came to a halt in front of the invader.

'Isla,' he greeted.

'I'd like a word.'

'Sure, why don't we go into the waiting area?'

'Why not your office?'

'I've sensitive items in there, and I'm no fool. Aileen Mackinnon sent ye.'

'She didn't,' came the indignant reply. 'I was here to ask if you found anything. No one in the town feels safe!'

'There's no need to be anxious. The police are here, aren't we? We've got it under control.'

'For all the good it did the dead tourist!'

Callan gave Isla a look, but she only shrugged.

As Isla left, Callan knew there was truth in what she'd said. Forced death had come to Loch Fuar after decades of welcomed drought. How could he assure the people that they were safe? And were they safe? He hadn't a clue.

CHAPTER EIGHT

Aileen rubbed her tired eyes. It had been a stressful day. The sullen atmosphere at the inn had turned almost macabre when a red-eyed Martha Smith had made an appearance in the evening.

On Samantha Grant's insistence, she managed to gulp down some chicken soup. Aileen had been tongue-tied, not knowing what to say, but she thought tomorrow would be far worse: it would have been Dave's birthday.

When Aileen had asked what they'd like for supper, almost everyone had said they hadn't the appetite. Legrand retired early, clearly displeased at being told to stay in Loch Fuar till the killer was caught. Apparently, he had urgent business in London.

Business more important than bringing the person responsible for a man's death to justice? Aileen scoffed. What a piece of work!

When everyone had retired to their respective bedrooms – a new one for Martha; one that hadn't been fully renovated yet – Aileen began to lock up. She checked the windows thrice this time; there was no room for errors.

But when it came to locking up the doors, it felt like a repeat of last night. She'd slipped the keys in her trousers' right pocket that morning, but once again she found herself patting the pocket – then squeezing it to make sure it was empty.

Her heart started beating frantically. No – not again! And then her hand landed on her left pocket. There – she heard the jingle of keys – and a grateful breath whooshed out of her lips.

But Aileen drew her eyebrows together; she could have sworn she'd put the keys in her right pocket.

She'd picked them off her nightstand with her right hand and heard them tinkling as she'd slipped them in. She hardly ever used her left pocket…

Aileen sighed. She must be remembering wrong. The day had been a strange one. She rubbed her fingers over the dull ache in her head. When would she learn to handle emotions: not just hers but others as well? They simply drained her empty.

And as an innkeeper, having a high emotional intelligence would stand her in good stead. Just like her ability to work ungodly hours. But sometimes this job seemed tougher than her former one.

Aileen's shoulders spasmed, a yawn slipping out of her lips.

No, Aileen. We need to investigate, she urged herself on.

An hour longer, she promised herself and sat with her computer in the small room adjacent to her bedroom. She'd converted the space into a study of sorts.

It didn't seem that tiny, but when Callan had stood in here asking questions, he'd looked like he was standing in a child's playhouse.

There were books piled on shelves behind her, and a few boxes she'd yet to sort through, plus some memorabilia her friends had brought back for her from their trips. Aileen had always wanted to travel, but there had been so many obstacles, like her job and her ambition.

Shaking these tangential thoughts, she peered at her notes. An entire afternoon of digging had got her nowhere. She hadn't found anything about the Dave Smith that had stayed at her inn. There wasn't any picture on the internet, nor was there an address.

She'd headed straight towards a dead end. Maybe it was time to try another line of investigation. She turned the events of last night over in her mind again.

The doors had been locked; there had been no windows broken. What were the chances that the killer was an outsider?

Absolutely none. It had to be one of her guests. Aileen shuddered to think she housed a murderer.

Had she heard him last night? But how could she be sure it was a man and not one of her female guests?

Aileen rubbed her forehead again. She needed another approach. Maybe…

Her thoughts abruptly halted as a shrill scream reverberated through the old walls of the inn. The sound was so piercing, so unexpected, that Aileen slapped her hands over her ears. Her heart thudded against her throat in abject terror.

The screaming continued like a call from hell. The snap of the chair smacking on the floor was barely audible as Aileen made a beeline for the stairs and ran down as fast as she could, trying her best not to break her neck.

The entire inn seemed to be in an uproar. Doors leading up to the guest rooms scraped opened, slammed shut; someone shouted. It was chaos.

Just like that morning, when an entirely different scream had shaken them all.

'What's the alarm for!' a voice shouted at her.

'Is this the bloody time for a drill?' That was John Cook.

Another wave of terror hit her. Who'd sounded the alarm? Why was it ringing? Was it a distraction?

The killer. Had he – had he struck again? She shivered as the chill ran through every nerve in her body. No, she warned her system, now was not the time to go completely lax with cold horror.

With a firm shake of her head, she took charge: of her body and her surroundings.

'The drawing room – now!' she bellowed above the alarm, like the slap of a whip.

Footsteps tumbled haphazardly over the wooden stairs, and Aileen crossed over to the Control Room and scampered to shut off the alarm.

The police would be here soon but first, she had to make sure everyone was accounted for.

A plethora of facial emotions greeted her in the drawing room: some sleepy, some annoyed, some confused, some even terrified or angry.

'Is this a joke? After what we've been through this morning, an alarm—'

Aileen's resolute hand stopped Richard Grant's rambling complaints. She looked around and sighed with relief: nine faces stared back at her.

The roar of a car's engine splintered the fragile glass of calm.

Before whoever it was broke down her front door, she yanked it open to find an irritated yet slightly concerned Detective Inspector Cameron.

'A false alarm,' she began to inform him as Callan pushed past her.

Like Aileen, he silently assessed the nine faces. And then, as one, her guests began...

'It's sinister! You can't...'

'Allow us to leave!'

'Woken up, out of our beds...'

Words like 'frightened', 'horrid' and 'unsafe' were splashed around.

Detective Inspector Callan Cameron surveyed the scene like a general before battle: adamant and superior.

When the volley of complaints finally subsided, he turned to Aileen. 'Show me the alarm.'

He didn't look like someone woken out of bed, Aileen thought as she led him upstairs to the control room. He was dressed in his standard black; the man owned no other colours it seemed.

'Control room?' he asked, reading the nailed wooden plate on the door.

'It's where we keep old security footage, registers and documents.'

'Seriously?' His voice held some disbelief as he pointed at the door. 'Ye store important documents in an unlocked room?'

'Who'd steal old registers?'

'Or security camera footage?' came the sarcastic reply.

Only Callan could be in the mood to start a fight at this time of night.

'Look at what you want to. I'll be upstairs.'

'Hold on.' He raised his hands. 'Tell me about the system.'

'It's an alarm,' Aileen informed him.

She didn't know much beyond that it was an alarm, but admitting that would make it look like she didn't know what she was doing, and she was certain he still thought she was a daft wee city girl, out of her depth. She had no desire to prove his theory right.

'It's an alarm system for the front and back door.' She shrugged. 'And the windows I think.' She mumbled the last part.

Callan dismissed her and set about investigating.

THE INSPECTOR SURVEYED THE TINY CLOSET-LIKE ROOM, cataloguing the heaps of papers and the different pieces of equipment. No one had come into the inn, as per the security footage. And there were no anomalies to be found in the footage either – no time losses or any sign of hacking.

But the alarm had sent an alert to the station. He'd still been in his office, puzzling over his incident board.

Callan pushed his hands into his jean pockets. Someone was getting desperate. But not desperate enough to leave clues.

A question knocked hard on his consciousness: had the alarm been a red herring or was it an unsuccessful attempt at another murder?

IT WAS WELL PAST MIDNIGHT WHEN CALLAN LEFT, AND everyone had gone back to bed. It was only then that Aileen found herself back at her desk.

The hope she'd catch some shut-eye was futile. Her mind raged with questions, the need to find answers more pressing than ever.

She didn't require forensic or autopsy reports to get to the bottom of this; she needed data on her guests. Whether it was numbers or letters, Aileen had a knack of finding discrepancies; falsified records always held some loose threads.

Her smile was confident. If there was one thing she knew was her superpower, it was her ability to find information no one wanted found, so with the strum of instrumental music in the background, Aileen began digging into the lives of each of her guests.

Her research began first with the most suspicious of the lot: Mr Louis Legrand. Unlike her murdered guest, Legrand was a well-known man, with too much wealth to count the zeros, and she found several articles written about him and his work.

Legrand was a preferred jeweller for the ultra-rich, and in his long career, he'd closed some lucrative deals involving all sorts of exotic jewelled items. According to one article, he was a ruthless negotiator and excellent at attaining artefacts his clients wanted at auction, at the best price.

He oozed cold-heartedness like juice out of a taut fruit.

Jean Beaulieu, the spouse, was an interesting man. A few articles spoke about the couple: Beaulieu had majored in geology before meeting Legrand. He'd been a professor at a university in France.

His geology background with expertise in precious stones would certainly be helpful to Legrand. And yes, Beaulieu had proved to be an asset.

Aileen drummed her fingers. Being skilled with jewels didn't make them murderers. They were what most would call a power couple, running a successful business together.

Aileen moved on to John Cook. He was another peculiar man... Did being an introvert – assuming he was one – mean a person wasn't compassionate? No. Aileen herself was one, and though she wasn't overly fond of people, she helped when they needed it.

John hadn't been rude like Legrand. In fact, he hadn't spoken a word voluntarily to her. Perhaps he was just the shy sort. She dismissed his behaviour and focused on the search results.

He was a family lawyer. It hadn't been hard to find out about him. He had his own practice and volunteered at a shelter during his free time. There was one news article about his contribution to a woman's shelter; he was a big campaigner against domestic violence.

Aileen played host to a wide spectrum of guests...

John Cook, the article told her, had also served some rich people. He too had the potential to be a target, especially if someone was holding a personal vendetta.

His partner, Susan Knight, was a female rights activist. She volunteered at the same shelter he did and had been doing so for fifteen-odd years; the official page of the shelter listed her laurels.

She moved her search to Martha Smith and came up with nothing. Dave had said the first – or was it the second? – night that she loved designing. A homemaker, that's what Dave had told the Grants she was.

Aileen stifled a yawn. The insistent dull throbbing in her forehead had turned into the loud smacks of a hammer on iron.

It was late in the night, almost dawn.

She turned the music off and crawled into bed, but not before making sure her keys were still in place.

Clasping her hands together, she prayed to any power who'd listen to get her out of this horridness as soon as possible – safely.

CALLAN HAD NO SUCH PRAYERS TO OFFER AS HE WORKED tirelessly in his office. No other case had captured his attention like this one. Indeed, it had been a while since he'd been this passionate about anything.

Maybe murder was a sombre affair— a man had lost his life— but a major part of him was glad to have a challenging job at long last!

He'd almost written a resignation letter after the last botched robbery he'd dealt with. Thieves in Loch Fuar were pathetic. And crime was minimal. He was fed up being an inspector in the land of saints.

It was seventh heaven having a murder to solve where the boss gave you full freedom – as long as you remain within budget. It was a damned thing, and rightly so, that Loch Fuar had such a lean budget that he could barely drink a glass of whisky every day for a year with it.

When a yawn wrenched his lips apart and he couldn't find the energy to brew another cup of coffee, Callan decided to call it a night.

Taking the police department's advice, he decided it was safest for the town that he crashed on the sofa in the waiting room. He would wake up as stiff as a creaky old corpse but to hell with it! It was nothing a good morning workout won't solve.

And with that thought, he went under, back into the nightmares that never left him.

DOZING ON A SOFA ENTIRELY TOO SHORT FOR HIS SIX-FOOT-plus height in the waiting room of the police station was the last place Aileen imagined she'd find Detective Inspector Callan Cameron.

Judging by the drool, he'd spent the night on that sofa.

'Aileen Mackinnon!' A tall man with unkempt white hair walked towards her. Callan's boss: Rory Macdonald. Her grandmother's friend and informant as well, Aileen recalled.

He pointed a stubby finger at the detective inspector. 'I thought about smacking his head, just to see how he reacted.'

'Aye?' Aileen raised an eyebrow.

'Aye.' With a satisfied smile he stuck his hands in his pockets. 'But he has circles under his eyes so I let it go. But you're here. For him?'

At her nod, he continued, 'Now I can smack him.' And he did.

Callan yelped, and like a panther woken from a deep sleep, he jumped off the sofa, ready to strike.

Rory boomed with laughter. 'Oh, lad!'

Aileen inwardly smirked. How she wished she'd had a boss like this before she'd become her own boss! Rory was fun!

With a wave, he left a stunned Callan and an amused Aileen Mackinnon alone. Laughter followed him out.

In the reception-cum-waiting-room, Aileen studied the blinking detective inspector. He looked out of sorts: red marks ran across his left cheek, his black shirt looked rumpled and his hair was tousled enough to look like Einstein's.

'No doubt he's off to scheme with yer gran.' Callan muttered under his breath.

Aileen knew her gran was tight with Rory. They had their old yet sharp ears pressed to the ground when it came to the town gossip.

'Um, I had something to discuss with you,' she began cautiously. The detective inspector looked furious and she needed his co-operation.

Callan folded his arms. 'What?'

Clearing her throat, Aileen told him about Legrand and Beaulieu.

'You see, from what I found, I think we can,' she sent up a quick prayer for luck, 'we can work together.'

When he remained silent, simply staring at her, Aileen supplied, 'I can help you find the murderer.'

All he did was snort, like a buffalo. 'Thanks, but I've got it. I'm the inspector.'

'But I have—'

He waved his hands. 'I'll get on with the case. It's got all my attention. Ye and yer guests will soon be free to leave. Everyone but the killer – he or she will be in prison,' Callan said in a gruff voice.

Clearly, a partner was the last thing he wanted.

'I know how to uncover information and find hidden facts,' Aileen countered.

All he did was shrug. 'This isn't a Miss Marple novel. You were at the inn when Smith was murdered. If ye haven't figured it out, let me inform you.' He pointed two fingers at Aileen. 'Ye are a suspect.'

A SUSPECT! AILEEN RAGED. SHE SLAPPED HER HAND ON THE car's steering wheel.

How dare he! Here she was, trying to help, and he dared to call her a suspect. Of course, she'd realised that *officially* she was, but to have it thrown at her like that, as if it might be true…

Aileen had tucked her tail between her legs and left immediately, while Callan had stormed into his office and slammed the door shut behind him – so hard that the entire station heard it.

Aileen squared her shoulders. If he wouldn't listen, she wasn't afraid to snoop around on her own. Adventurous Aileen was up for it.

But before she could get down to it, her innkeeper's duties were calling her. It was breakfast hour.

Aileen returned to the inn before her guests were up. She didn't know why, but she'd assumed Callan would be at the station early this morning. He looked like someone who enjoyed his work.

Little could she have predicted he'd spent the night there.

Dachaigh was as quiet as she'd left it. None of her guests were up yet.

Isla, however, waited at the kitchen counter. 'Where have you been?'

She knew she had a confidante in Isla, so Aileen told her: about her research, the false alarm and her morning rendezvous, which had failed in epic proportions.

'I'm worried, Isla,' Aileen sighed. 'I got an email from a guest cancelling their stay. They were heading out here to celebrate their anniversary. An old couple from the next town.'

'It's just a bump in the road. Things'll be fine soon.'

'The sooner the better – I don't know how long I can afford a drop in revenue.'

'Bah!' Isla waved her off. 'Don't start with that accounting jargon.'

'I'll need to cut expenditures to stay afloat. And the cash flow…' Aileen ended up laughing at Isla's agonised expression.

Despite being the owner of a bakery, Isla didn't believe number crunching was necessary for a successful business. She'd told Aileen time and again to have faith – in her business and her customers. And herself.

Their laughter died out when Martha Smith approached. As then, like a funeral procession, the rest of the guests followed.

As her guests sat down for breakfast, the cuckoo clock announced the morning hour. And a refreshing aroma of fresh bread, omelettes and baked beans swirled through the miserable room.

Martha slid into a chair. 'Could you make some banana pancakes, please? He loved them,' she mumbled before breaking down into fits of sadness.

Weeping followed sniffles which turned into melancholy. And just like that, breakfast became a sombre affair.

CHAPTER NINE

When Rory Macdonald tapped on his office door, Callan had fully woken up. Coming out of sleep to find Aileen and his boss laughing at his expense had downright annoyed him.

He'd changed out of his rumpled shirt now – like all hardworking inspectors, he had a spare set of clothes with him – and had dumped a steaming cup of bitter coffee down his throat. It was only because of this that he nodded a greeting at Rory.

'Working hard I see,' Rory drawled.

Callan shrugged. 'We haven't had a murder here for a while and local folks would like to see its back already.'

'They naturally feel a bit scared.' Rory scrutinised the incident board. 'Ye know something about murder and its brutality. That's why ye've got this case.'

Callan nodded. 'I dug into our records as well as internet records – there seems to be no sign of our Dr Dave Smith,' he explained. 'So I contacted the car rental service they hired to get here. Waiting on a response; it's still early yet.'

Rory analysed the board and ran a hand through his white mop. Suddenly he turned his sharp eyes on the inspector.

'When I hired ye, yer file said ye had a history of working alone. Now, I'm not about to delve into the why, but,' he narrowed his eyes, 'I think ye could use a little help with this one.'

Callan's intense eyes turned determined. 'I've got this. I'll find the killer. And I work best alone – I don't need anyone to come down from—'

He stopped when Rory shook his head. 'I'm not suggesting ye call another detective inspector.' Placing both his hands in his pockets, Rory continued, 'Aileen Mackinnon – she'd be an asset.'

The innkeeper? That was the last person Callan had thought his boss would suggest.

'Sir, with all due respect, she's the innkeeper and a suspect.'

'Callan, here's where ye're wrong. Aileen Mackinnon has no motive, does she?'

'We don't know much about her. She's come here from the city, out of the blue. Why?'

'Why not ask her?'

Callan shrugged. 'She was an accountant!' That ought to do it!

'A *forensic* accountant!' Rory said slowly as if making a point.

He continued, 'Her job required her to dig into data, find anomalies. She's good at IT, good at numbers and very good at finding the sorts of things that the killer might want hidden.'

All he could do was sigh. What Rory said made some sense but working with Aileen? He wasn't sure.

'I'll consider it,' he conceded.

With his hands in his pockets, Rory left.

Callan approached his ancient computer. Who was Aileen Mackinnon? If he was to partner with her, he'd have to find out.

AILEEN HAD NO IDEA WHAT TO DO. SHE'D FOUND OUT A LOT of information; not about Dave Smith, but about Louis Legrand and his French spouse, but the rest of them… Aileen drummed her fingers on the old wooden desk. The rest of them were tricky. If only, the thick-headed inspector had agreed to team up – with his resources she'd get to the bottom of this pretty quick.

She could smell it, feel it like it was something tangible: the lie that had been woven around this entire situation. With some information, she'd be able to pick out the threads of truth.

Aileen almost jumped out of her chair when her phone buzzed. It was a text from Callan.

Come down to the station.

It was with sheer amazement that she raised her brows. That was unexpected.

Maybe she had got through that thick skull after all. Maybe she could wipe out the black spell cast on her Dachaigh.

Maybe you could move out the door first, she chided herself as she packed up.

It took her ten minutes to fly out the door, cover the distance into town and find a place to park. She didn't want to spread suspicion, so she parked in front of Isla's bakery, waving her friend off – she'd tell her what was going on later – and walked towards the police station.

There weren't many people around, despite it being a

Monday. Aileen smiled – small-town charm. Maybe adventure was what she'd readied herself for, but the slow life was what she'd wanted.

She walked on down the street, slowing as she came to an old brick building with a small iron sign jutting out from it. The iron had been curved to show a cup of tea. The wooden sign hanging over the brown wooden door read: Barbara's Tea Room.

Would Isla be interested in joining her here for a cuppa later? Aileen gazed fondly through the window. Everything was cast in a beautiful cosy golden light.

There were people inside, Aileen noted, and was that? Surely not.

Aileen peered in as inconspicuously as she could, and yes – sitting inside were Jean Beaulieu and Richard Grant, having some sort of a conversation.

A serious conversation, Aileen observed. They hunched towards each other as if sharing secrets. What could they be doing here together?

Aileen shook her head. It was something to note down, but there was no point in reading too much into it yet.

She picked up her pace as the street curved round towards the police station. It was just as she'd found it that morning – quiet as a telegram office.

'Inspector Cameron,' she greeted him, the fragrance of coffee hitting her as she stepped inside.

CALLAN TOOK HIS TIME, SIPPING THE COFFEE HE'D JUST brewed and assessing Aileen from under his lashes.

He wasn't sure they'd work out as a team, but he'd realised that if he wanted to solve this case quickly, he'd need an assistant. And from the research he'd done on her – the *extensive* research – he'd found out she was good at her job.

There'd been an article about how she'd gone out of her way to investigate the financial anomalies of a company she'd been assigned to audit. She'd found what her bosses hadn't, essentially exposing a big fraud.

He wanted to ask her why she'd left such a successful career behind, but Callan didn't get personal. All he cared about was that they found the killer.

'Ye're here quick.'

'The sooner we get this done, the better.'

Callan nodded and let out a long breath. 'Ye came here this morning to discuss the case – do ye have any data?'

'Are you agreeing to let me help in the investigation?'

Callan wasn't sure but he said, 'I'd like the data.'

'I'd like an assurance that you won't steal my data.'

'Don't argue with me.' Callan's temper shone through.

Aileen held her ground and gave him a look. 'We'll work together. You need my skills, I know. You're short-staffed. And you've got access to records. I need your resources,' she deadpanned.

Callan looked away. He didn't have time to argue with a stubborn woman.

'We have a computer in that room. No one uses it.' It seemed like a good way to start this pseudo partnership. Callan had no interest in sharing his thoughts about the investigation with her – she was still a suspect as far as he was concerned.

Though, if he was honest, he thought it was unlikely she was the killer. To encourage such a scandal attached to her inn, which she'd just spent a cartload of money to renovate, seemed like self-sabotage.

Or a good marketing gimmick.

The computer room was smaller than a closet and windowless. The room offered no distractions.

A desk that looked older than Arthur's round table sat against one wall, along with a chair more ancient than the Celts, and Callan caught Aileen rolling her eyes when her gaze fell on the computer, which in all fairness did look like the first prototype Charles Babbage might have created.

'First,' Callan said as he led Aileen back into his office, 'tell me what ye know.' He'd turned the incident board around before she'd arrived and stuffed his files into an empty drawer in the cabinet by his desk.

He watched as she assessed his office, her eyes lingering on the papers peeking out of the drawers as if seeing such a lack of organisation pained her. Then her gaze moved to the turned around incident board and she smirked. 'Don't inspectors make incident boards?'

She caught on quick, Callan thought, but he merely shrugged.

'As my partner, you need to share too, you know,' Aileen reminded him.

'Ye tell me first, partners or not. I'm the inspector – the one in-charge.'

Fair enough, Aileen seemed to concede as she sat down quietly on the uncomfortable visitor's chair. She didn't want to risk pissing him off.

'You've got to share too. Just remember that.' Callan heard her mutter.

When she was done setting up her personal computer, Aileen began her 'presentation'.

'Louis Legrand,' she explained, 'is a jeweller who caters to the ultra-rich. He's done some major trades…' Aileen explained it all to him then moved on to the husband.

'Beaulieu was a professor before. And now they have a successful business together. Legrand started it; Beaulieu contributed to it. No over the top, scandalous controversies, though there are some complaints, as you'd expect.'

Callan stood by the window, staring out. He was paying close attention to what Aileen was telling him, even if he wasn't looking at her. She'd found out a lot in such a short amount of time and with the meagre resources she had. Maybe she could be an asset after all.

'So what can you tell me?' she asked.

Callan cast a pointed look at her. 'Finish what you started first. What about the other guests? Dave Smith himself?'

Aileen pursed her lips. 'That's the catch. I've got zip on Dave Smith. He doesn't exist!'

Callan nodded and gave her a wide smile; Aileen narrowed her eyes. 'What?'

'We have nothing on him. There are a few Dave Smiths in the system – it's a common name, after all – but nothing that matches the dead man. There's no match for his DNA either.'

Callan gestured for Aileen to finish her piece.

'John Cook,' she continued. 'He's a lawyer and a volunteer at a woman's shelter. His partner, Susan Knight is a female rights activist and also works at the shelter. I think they met there.'

'Where did you get information about Cook and Knight from?'

'The official website of the shelter. I was about to call them before you texted. It's a Monday so they should be open for business.'

Callan nodded.

'The Grants and Martha Smith: they're a challenge,'

Aileen continued. 'I found nothing on the Canadians or the new widow. There's no name match, nor anything about their gallery. They were talking about it at dinner one night.'

'They spoke about their professions?'

'Yes, the night Smith was alive.'

'Hmmm.' Callan tapped his chin thoughtfully. 'And Martha Smith?'

Aileen shrugged. 'Same as her husband – it's like she doesn't exist.'

Callan nodded again. He had to stick to his word now. He walked over to the incident board and turned it around to face his new… Partner.

He'd done a thorough job, listing every last detail he knew, and he watched as she studied it all carefully. She looked vaguely disturbed at seeing her own face on the board, but her expression changed when she got to the photos of the murder scene. She'd seen it first-hand of course, but a lot of the detail had probably been lost in the aftermath of her shock.

'It's always so vague in the movies. Not that much… Destruction,' she observed, swallowing. Her skin had turned pale.

'It's not the movies. Ye have to deal with it.' Callan had thrown up a week's worth of food the first time he'd seen the devastation deliberate death caused. But now, no emotions tickled his throat. It was almost as if the murder was normal, as much of a fact as breathing.

He angled the board and pointed at a photo of Dave Smith's cleaned pale face on the medical examiner's steel table.

'That's the only picture of him we have. According to the report from the medical examiner, he died at around 3 a.m. We ran him for data, including fingerprints, and as I said before – nada, not a single name.' Callan sighed. 'The facial recognition software might take some more time.'

Aileen digested the information before she spoke. 'Is this search across the UK?'

'Pretty much, but we focused more on Scotland.'

'And Martha?' Aileen questioned.

Callan didn't answer; Aileen gulped, clearly unsettled.

Both of them turned quiet then, thinking.

'You said the murder took place after three in the morning,' Aileen said eventually. 'Does that mean the foot-steps I heard are irrelevant?'

'You're the only one who heard them.'

'That's preposterous! They were muffled, not loud enough to wake someone up, but there were ten other people in that inn and you expect me to believe not a single one heard anything?'

Callan snorted out a laugh at that. 'Something to keep in mind, aye? Ye should've heard them the next day. Humbugs the lot of them, I say.'

'What do you mean?'

'I can spot a liar from a mile away. And all of them lied.' He fixed Aileen with a stare. 'And so did you.'

'Me?'

'Aye.'

'I didn't lie,' Aileen retorted with a shake of her head.

'Maybe "withheld information" would be the correct phrase?' Callan was enjoying himself. The prim and proper innkeeper might be good at detection but she was pathetic at lying.

Why, wasn't she sitting there now, blushing red and squirming in her seat!

Aileen seemed to battle with herself for a moment and then gave in – for the sake of their partnership he supposed.

'I didn't think it was relevant at the time,' she began to explain. 'It didn't make sense either.'

She jingled a pair of keys in her pocket.

'I've always been a responsible person, never lost a thing. But that day, when I was locking up, I couldn't find my keys to start with.'

Callan stuffed his hands in his pockets. 'That's unusual?'

'It's a ritual. That's how I never forget. Living in the city, I always locked everything before heading to bed. I'm extra particular about the keys. I have them on me at all times, like now.' She patted her right pocket. 'But that night, I couldn't find them at all. I looked everywhere. Eventually, I found them at the reception counter.'

'So?' Callan asked.

'I'd never do that! The reception is near the front door. I'd never keep the keys out for everyone to see, especially when I have to account for the safety of ten other people.'

'You're a safety freak?' Callan mocked her. The pitiful number of security cameras she'd installed sure hadn't given him that impression!

'It's a habit my mother instilled in me as a child. We'd always lock up and she taught me to keep keys away from areas in the house where other people could easily access them.'

Callan considered for a moment. 'Where did ye remember last seeing them?'

'I could've sworn I dropped them into my right trouser pocket that morning.'

After a moment of hesitation, Aileen added, 'It happened again. Not so drastic but after the murder – that night – I found them in my left pocket. But I remember slipping them into my right.'

'What sort of keys do you have on the ring?'

'All of them.' Aileen twiddled her fingers. 'I know, for someone crazy about keys, I don't take enough security measures.'

'You think? You've barely installed security cameras, you've got a room with sensitive data like the security tapes with no lock and you carry your keys with you everywhere!'

'Why would someone pickpocket my keys? Dachaigh is an inn, not a bank!'

Callan ordered himself to remain calm. 'Data is the new currency, Aileen. Ye surely don't need me to tell ye that. And an inn has data from their guests.'

She looked like she hadn't considered that.

'Have ye got a safe in the inn?' he continued.

She nodded. 'It's Siobhan's. I haven't opened it up for a while.'

By the time Aileen left his office to work on the other computer, Callan's head ached with rage.

You could be a novice, you could be naïve, but who in their right mind thought like Aileen? She'd not even thought about the safe! And when he'd suggested she should have a look, she'd said she'd do so that night.

But in his gut, Callan knew it was already too late.

He looked at the incident board. The best way to get through the rage and get some time to think was to work out. Lord knew he needed the physical exertion.

His day had begun and remained as shitty as it could get.

A SHORT WHILE LATER, CALLAN WAS JOGGING THROUGH the old narrow streets of Loch Fuar.

As he rounded a corner, he saw them: Susan Knight

and Samantha Grant — or at least that's what they'd called themselves. They stood outside the bakery, looking at the bread inside. They said something to each other in hushed voices, then one of them cast a slanted look Callan's way.

Abruptly, they turned as one and walked briskly in the opposite direction.

What was going on?

Callan hissed out a breath and continued down the street.

Susan Knight and Samantha Grant — what did they have in common except that they were lodging at the same inn at the same time? Were they friends?

Callan panted as he increased his pace. His right leg protested, but as always he ignored the dull ache.

Mingling with people wasn't his forte. He liked to stay away from anything that could breathe and speak. But he knew, no matter what, a sane person wouldn't associate themselves with a stranger at an inn where a murder had just taken place.

He had to look into it — or perhaps Aileen could. She was much better placed to keep an eye on her guests.

An hour later, he was calm and truly at peace. The positive energy gave him the gusto to add to his incident board: Aileen's information about her guests as well as the big question plaguing him — the relationships between them all.

AILEEN'S BODY CRAMPED AS SHE BLINKED AND STRETCHED. This chair was so uncomfortable! And this computer. She rolled her eyes.

Perhaps it would be best if she used her phone. That way her tired eyes could take a break.

Would it help to call the shelter? Or would John and Susan call her out if they found out she'd been snooping?

She worried her lips, contemplating.

No, Aileen! she told herself firmly. Adventurous, courageous; it was time to follow her mantra now.

Tapping her fingers on the old desk, she dialled the shelter's number.

The phone rang once and her heart told her 'abort mission'. On the second ring, her heart told her 'this is a bad idea'. On the third, her heart began thudding in her chest.

What if she irritated her guests more than they already were?

They were under investigation, for God's sake! They had to be annoyed. And her business! She didn't—

'Queen Mary's Shelter for Women,' came a kind voice.

Aileen took a breath. 'Hello.'

'Hello! How may I help you?'

'Ah, um...' Aileen shut her eyes and took a breath. 'I, um, my friend wanted help.'

She hated lying but she had to. Her fingers drummed so fast she could barely see them.

'Help, Miss? Can you tell me what you mean by that?'

Aileen had to go with the flow. 'Yes, my friend. Um, she says it's nothing but I saw bruises on her yesterday. She doesn't come to our weekly yoga lessons anymore either – says she's preoccupied. I know she'd never missed those. And,' Aileen sent a prayer up to apologise for the deception, 'she flinched when she saw her husband the other day. We were in the supermarket—'

Flinched when she saw her husband... Who'd done that? Aileen could swear she'd seen it happen. That wasn't her imagination. Last night? In the—

'We can help your friend out, Miss...?'

'McHugh!' Aileen hissed out the last part. Terrible! She was terrible at lying! 'I wanted Ms Knight to help my friend. I read on your website she consults?'

The person on the other side of the line seemed kind enough. 'Ms Knight? Yes, she's one of the best we've got.'

'And John Cook? Um, he's the lawyer, yes?'

'Mr Cook?' The lady hesitated. 'That's a little tricky to arrange, Ms McHugh.'

'Tricky?'

'Yes, um, the two of them don't work cases together anymore. In fact…' The lady cleared her throat and whispered, 'Mr Cook doesn't work much with our shelter either these days.'

'Why?'

'I shouldn't be saying this but, for your friend…' The lady had gone into gossip mode. After a pause, she whispered, 'They've been involved romantically for many years and you know how most of those things end.'

'Oh.' Aileen's surprise was truly genuine.

'Yes,' the lady continued, 'I don't know the details but there was some kind of fight and now the two don't work together, and Mr Cook doesn't come in much.'

Aileen frowned as she rang off. She'd told the kind lady she needed to consult her friend again before wasting the shelter's time.

The call had paid off. But where did the information lead them? A domestic feud had nothing to do with Dave Smith. She'd think about it later; for now, she had to get back to the inn.

CALLAN WAS ENGROSSED IN HIS WORK, GLARING AT THE

report from the forensic team. Their sweep had turned up nothing.

At a soft knock on his door, Callan turned around to find Aileen. Callan frowned at her wide eyes. Before he could ask what was wrong, she said, 'Someone slashed my tyres!'

CHAPTER TEN

Slashed had been a kind word. Someone had destroyed her car tyres – all of them.

'I'm so sorry. I thought if I got everything sorted in the bakery, I could come and visit you later.' Isla had come out of her shop after hearing all the commotion. 'I didn't see anyone by your car but,' she sighed, 'I was in the back, baking. No one comes over before I bake the latest batch. And we have no leftovers to sell either!'

'When's that? You sell your latest batch at...' Callan interrupted.

'Five sharp – and always have.'

Callan glanced at his watch; it was nearly five. But there weren't many people around.

'It was alright when I passed by earlier,' he observed.

He was naturally observant anyway, but his training had made him exemplary. Anything out of the ordinary would have drawn his attention immediately. He thought briefly about Susan Knight and Samantha Grant but they didn't look like the sort to do this. Besides they'd fled after he'd seen them together. What was that about?

'CCTV footage?' he asked Isla.

'You can check it out, although I'm afraid it doesn't look out on the car, just the front door from this angle.'

The last thing Callan needed was for his time to be taken up by mindless security-footage hunting.

Why slash the innkeeper's tyres? Was it a local irked that she was here running the inn? Or was it one of the guests?

'I'll fix you two a coffee and some cake I just baked while you look through the footage.'

But as Isla had predicted, the car was too far away to be seen on the footage.

It had been a bold move, slashing someone's tyres in broad daylight in the busier part of town.

'They had the local vendors' meeting today at Barbara's,' Isla explained. 'I didn't go but the rest went. Daniel said he'd fill me in.'

Well, that explained the lack of people. Damn hard luck!

AILEEN SAT DEJECTED AND STILL THE WHOLE WAY BACK TO the inn. Callan had offered to drop her off and Isla had agreed with him, saying it was best he saw to it that she got back safely.

Aileen hadn't bothered to rebuke her friend for meddling.

She wondered whether this adventurous foray into the Highlands had been too much for her. The slashed tyres were definitely a warning. But who knew she'd teamed up with the inspector to hunt the killer?

She shuddered to think how far the killer might go to keep her away.

'You don't need me to tell ye to be careful,' Callan informed her as he pulled up in front of Dachaigh.

She'd been quiet, understandably so. But there was a lot he had to consider.

First and foremost was that whoever had done this had to have known about the vendors' meeting – and that Aileen wasn't attending.

Perhaps someone had wanted to delay her return to the inn. But who? And why?

At this moment, all Callan could do was warn her. He trailed behind her as Aileen walked up the driveway.

She tried brushing him off. 'I got it.'

Callan simply followed her inside.

The golden lights of the reception area were warm and welcoming, and Callan remembered the first night he'd visited the inn. Siobhan had stood behind the counter, her hair as white as snow, and flashed him a smile as warm as the sun.

He looked at Siobhan's granddaughter now. Both these women had one thing in common: they were deceptively strong. Most people would have created a scene by now, given everything that had happened, but she'd remained calm.

'Since I'm here, I'll have a look in the control room,' Callan informed Aileen as he made his way up the stairs.

Light shone under some of the guest rooms. His shoes made no sound on the carpeted floor, his steps light.

He heard a muffled sound from one bedroom.

'I don't know!' came a high-pitched terrified voice. It was definitely male.

Callan's feet halted, his ears perking up.

A gruff voice retorted. 'You made that deal! Remember?'

'You can't possibly think—'

'Hadn't I asked you to research?'

'I did!'

'I'm done with this. I'm telling you, warning you,' a hard, furious voice whispered. It was so low, Callan had to inch towards the door to hear it. 'If we don't get this deal, I'm going to the police.'

There was a moment of silence. 'What do you mean?'

'I know what you did.'

'But – but I sold it!' the alarmed voice countered.

The sounds abruptly halted as footsteps echoed off the walls, heading his way. Callan jumped away. Someone was coming up the stairs.

He quickly turned into the adjacent corridor and peered back into the one he'd just left.

Jean Beaulieu walked up and disappeared into a room. The guest room where he'd heard the voices remained quiet; no one entered or exited.

When everything had been calm for a few minutes, Callan went into the control room. It had been as he'd seen it the first time. Nothing missing, apart for the security footage he'd taken with him to the station.

Abruptly he turned and walked back down the stairs to the reception desk, and looked at the registry, rechecking what he'd already seen.

Scratching his day's scruff, he thought about the conversation he'd overheard.

He was frowning, deep in thought when a pot clanged. It was followed by a curse. He knew that voice.

With a roll of his eyes, Callan walked into the aromatic kitchen.

'Who's staying in room four?' he asked without preamble.

Aileen muttered another curse – she was staring down at a very frozen chicken; perhaps it was supposed to have been dinner – before casting an exasperated glance at Callan. 'No one.'

'That can't be right. I heard someone up there.'

Aileen shrugged. 'Look, I'm busy here. You're the inspector. I know I haven't given room four to anyone. It's not finished.'

Before she could say anything else, Callan walked briskly up the stairs again, strode over to room four and pushed the door open.

Aileen had been right – it was unfinished. The bed frame stood without a mattress. The wallpaper had been ripped off, leaving behind ugly spots of glue, and a few paint and turpentine bottles rested against the wall.

So who'd been here before?

Callan walked to the sole lamp that stood on the only other piece of furniture in the room – a round table – and studied it. But he didn't touch it.

He looked around in the room, then checked the dilapidated bathroom. Not a soul and no way to escape. The room had no adjoining door leading into the next room either.

Callan looked into the closet and almost broke the door handle off.

Satisfied with his digging, he called PC Robert Davis, the only other policeman on the payroll apart from Rory.

'Get a kit to Dachaigh quick.'

He hung up and stood thinking in that dirty room as the sun began to call it a day. He'd never been one for sunsets; they made him feel sad.

As the waning sun cast long shadows in the room,

Callan folded his hands, stared at the stunning landscape of home and replayed the conversation he'd overheard. Thanks to his excellent memory he remembered it exactly.

Focus on the tone, he told himself.

One accusatory, one defiant – almost scared. What did the accusatory voice know? And what had the other person done?

The voices had both been rather tensed and a bit gruff. Male. And the accents? They were clearly English, closer to London to be precise.

A knock on the door made him turn around. Aileen stood there, and behind her was Robert.

Carefully he set the kit on the bed, then took out the brush and powder, handing them to Callan, who meticulously dusted the lamp switch.

He noted Aileen watching on in awe as he lifted a partial fingerprint. Thankfully, she didn't bombard him with questions.

Callan turned to Robert. 'Get this to the lab. Drive over now – say it's urgent. We need them to match it for us.'

'Got it.' Robert smiled at Aileen. 'See ya.' And with that, he dashed out. Robert had only just passed his police exam but Rory had taken him under his wing. Despite his young age and green disposition, Robert was diligent in his work.

'Care to explain what you found?' Ah, questions…

Callan looked at Aileen. 'When's dinner?'

When she only stared back at him, Callan shrugged. This partner thing was getting on his nerves!

He told her what he'd heard.

'And I saw a faint glow of light, so someone would have had to have switched the light on. We'll find out who it was soon enough.'

Aileen considered for a moment. 'Are you sure they had English accents? That's strange—'

Callan rolled his eyes. Did she think he was daft – or deaf? 'Yes – and ye do have three guests who are English, do ye not?'

'Yes, but only one of them is male,' she fired back.

Callan changed the subject. 'So, dinner?'

Within a few minutes, he sat enjoying a nice bowl of warm soup, with fresh bread.

None of her guests had made an appearance yet. So when Callan insisted, Aileen joined him with a cup of coffee.

'Won't you have trouble sleeping?' he asked.

'I don't plan on sleeping. I've got some things I need to check.'

Callan sighed. This woman was certainly impatient. 'Did you find something in the system this afternoon?'

'Sort of – I'm not exactly sure.'

At Callan's confused look, she elaborated, 'I was thinking about the murder weapon. It's a unique piece, the knife. Almost artistic – and antique.'

'So ye think it's something to do with the Grants?'

Aileen nodded. 'Perhaps, but you'll need evidence, won't you? So I thought we could try to identify who owned the piece and searched the internet for auction listings.'

The cuckoo clock chimed the evening hour, but still, none of her guests appeared for dinner.

When Callan gestured for her to continue, Aileen told him how she'd found a few potential matches in auction-eers' dailies and finally narrowed it down to two possibilities.

'What the dailies don't say is who purchased them. They were both silent auctions, held online, through an agent. Now you'd ask what the Grants have to do with it, but art dealers could also dabble in antiques, though there's no record of their business on the internet.'

'Right, and every business must have a presence online?'

'If not a business, at least the person behind it,' Aileen pressed her point. 'There's no mention of Richard, Samantha, Jacob or Anne Grant. At least none who look like the people staying at my inn.'

'How do you plan on finding out more about the dagger?'

But Callan's question remained unanswered when footsteps descended the stairs and Martha Smith walked up to the table. Contrary to the last couple of days, she looked put together.

She smiled and said, 'I didn't know you were here, Inspector.'

'Had some things I needed to cross-check. Say, Mrs Smith, what's your educational background?'

'Educational? Oh well, I studied Psychology.'

'Where?'

'Oh, um, nowhere you'd know,' Martha deflected the question.

'Edinburgh perhaps?' Callan pressed.

'A little ways from Edinburgh.'

Callan noticed she twiddled her thumbs and pulled at her jumper. That was what she'd done when he'd interviewed her, even though she'd been crying most of the time. A very prominent nervous tell. What was she nervous about?

'That's where you met your husband?'

At that intrusive question, Martha's lips trembled. She nodded her response with a slight bob of her head.

'Excuse me.' She jerked away and walked briskly out the room.

Aileen raised her brow in question. 'The least you could do is be kind to her.'

'She's done nothing but lie this entire time,' Callan defended himself. He wasn't an oaf. 'I'm just trying to figure out the truth.'

A WHILE LATER, CALLAN STOOD. 'THANKS FOR THE MEAL. And let me know what ye find about the knife.'

'Dagger – it was a dagger.'

Callan performed a mock salute and strode out.

He had a way of walking, Aileen mused. As if there was something not quite right with his right leg...

'Aileen.' Samantha Grant walked towards her and took her hand. 'Richard's feeling a bit under the weather; could you please fix a tray for him that I could take upstairs?'

'Sure.'

Aileen was done with all her chores by half-past nine, an incredible feat for an innkeeper who provided dinner for her guests. Though perhaps it was something to do with the lack of guests who ventured out of their rooms, Aileen thought, rolling her eyes.

Almost as if they'd heard her, Martha Smith and Anne Grant appeared on the stairs.

'Mrs Smith. Mrs Grant.' Aileen's smile was forced.

'Oh, we were just about to head to the drawing room!' Anne informed her.

Martha nodded. 'Yes, we discovered a joint interest in baking bread!' She laughed.

Anne waved a rectangular pouch. 'I've got recipes with me. We're sharing.'

On that happy note, the two walked down as Aileen went up.

Her rooms on the upper floor were as she'd left them. She sighed. She craved a bath, but the dagger was more important.

Perhaps hiring someone to cook would be a good idea – then she'd have more time to do research. She'd barely had a chance to think anything more about it since this afternoon...

Budget, came the flat response.

The phone buzzed; it was Callan.

'Hello.'

'Did you check your safe?'

'The safe? Oh! I completely forgot about it.'

'Check it right now,' Callan's voice boomed through the line.

She opened her closet, removed a drawer out and inserted the key in.

'It hasn't been used in forever. No one even knows about it except for Siobhan.'

Callan didn't respond.

The thick steel door took some effort to pull open. The safe was a tiny one, but Siobhan had come to Loch Fuar with very little.

Aileen studied the contents and smiled at the stack of letters her grandmother had preserved. She knew they were love letters from her grandpa.

And the dust-covered maroon box – the pseudo diamond engagement ring Aileen's father had told her about. The story had made Aileen's romantic heart sigh.

Her grandfather hadn't been a rich man, so he'd purchased a stone that looked like a diamond, designed the ring for his lady and then asked her to marry him.

'It's all in place,' she assured Callan.

'Are you sure? If there's jewellery, did you open the boxes?'

'Everything seems to be covered with a thick coating of dust. Won't there be fingerprints if someone had opened the safe?'

Callan's voice held annoyance. 'Open the boxes, Aileen.'

She sighed petulantly, frustrated. 'Hold on,' Aileen ordered as she balanced the phone between her shoulder and ear. Reaching for the dusty velvet box, she pulled it open.

Her gasp was loud down the phone.

'It's gone!' she cried. 'Gran's engagement ring is gone!'

CHAPTER ELEVEN

Aileen slumped on the door in front of her closet. What an idiot she had been!

Hadn't Aileen always vowed to trust herself? So when the keys weren't in their place, twice, she should have been suspicious. Besides—

Aileen gasped again. What had happened to the lights? She was cast in pitch darkness.

Aileen held her thoughts on a leash, calmed her mind and perked up her ears: everything was absolutely quiet. Noiselessly, she held the phone's torch in her hand and tiptoed to her room's door.

Her boots made muffled sounds on the carpeted floor, then an old plank creaked. It sounded loud in the hush of the night.

There was no other sound, no shouting to indicate the lights had abruptly gone off.

Squaring her shoulders, Aileen walked down the stairs.

A door at the far end of the corridor opened, and she paused.

Heavy footsteps strode towards the stairs, then a torch-light shone in the corridor.

The light beam came closer but Aileen couldn't see the person behind it.

'Hello?' Aileen cleared away the fear in her throat.

The torch jerked, followed by a curse before the voice spoke. 'Jake Grant. What's happened?'

'The lights went out. Let me head over to the main switches.'

Jake followed Aileen as she went into the control room.

Just then she heard a car drive up. It had to be Callan.

Sure enough, heavy footsteps soon raced up the stairs, and another brighter torch appeared and followed them.

'Everybody okay?' Callan asked.

Aileen cleared her parched throat; she had a bad feeling about this. 'I don't know. I was just about to check the fuse board.'

But Callan pushed ahead. 'Darn it! Looks like some-one's turned off the switch for the lights.'

'But the board's locked behind—'

The lights blinded them for a moment. Aileen opened her eyes to see Callan give her a look. He turned to Jake. 'Please head over to the library.'

Another set of footsteps came down the hall. John Cook appeared, and behind him came Martha Smith, along with Anne Grant.

John strode up to them. 'We were in the drawing room when the lights went out.'

Martha nodded. 'Yes, we thought the power must have tripped.'

Callan regarded them and caressed his scruff.

Jake pointed at Callan. 'He's asked us to wait in the library.'

When it was just the two of them, Aileen turned to Callan.

'Someone turned them off deliberately?'

Callan said not a word. The fuse board was indeed barricaded inside a locked cabinet. A consummate thief could click the lock open, but he had no doubt that whoever had done it had an entire set of keys. They didn't need to break in. And only the lights had gone off; the rest of the power had stayed on, so it didn't seem to be an electrical fault.

'It's not a red herring like yesterday's alarm,' Callan muttered. His intuition told him something had happened. They were too late.

'I'm going to knock on everyone's door. Assemble everyone in the library.'

'But…' Before she could argue that she was his partner, Callan was off.

CALLAN KNOCKED ON RICHARD AND SAMANTHA GRANT'S door first.

He couldn't hear a thing inside the room, and wasn't it odd that so many of them were in bed already? He glanced at his watch. It was barely half-past ten.

Callan knocked on the door again. This time there was some shuffling before a faint glow of light flickered from under the door and footsteps padded across the room. The door opened slightly and Richard Grant stuffed his face in the meagre crack that appeared.

'It's Detective Inspector Callan Cameron. Yer wife and ye safe?'

Richard's eyes looked around. 'What's wrong?'

'Yer wife?'

'What is it?' came a sleepy feminine voice he recognised as Samantha's.

'Please stay put.'

With that, he knocked on the next door. But it was already open a crack.

He knocked again loudly, but no one responded. Then the door next to it pulled open.

'What's all this hullabaloo?' Jean Beaulieu's heavily accented yet irritated voice halted Callan's knocking.

The door opened farther and an annoyed Louis Legrand stepped out in a jade-silk night robe.

'Don't we pay enough to get a peaceful night's sleep?'

'Who stays in this room?' Callan demanded, gesturing to the other door.

'Ask the innkeeper,' Legrand growled, muttering curses under his breath.

Samantha Grant cleared her throat. She and her husband now stood in their doorway. 'As far as I know, it's empty.'

'Room number nine,' Callan noted. Another empty room mystery.

'Stay put,' he repeated to both couples.

Drawing out his gun, he pushed open the door. The room was a dark abyss.

He took out his torch and flashed it around…

Callan's broad shoulders slumped, and he let out a breath between clenched teeth. Death had dipped its claws into Dachaigh again.

HE WENT IN, KICKING THE DOOR CLOSE BEHIND HIM AND assessed the scene. Just like room four, this one was unfinished, though the walls had been cleared of wallpaper and painted.

The closet doors were unhinged and rested against one wall, while the bathroom was untiled and unfinished. Like room four, there was a bed frame with no mattress on it, but this time there was no lamp.

Satisfied that there was no one around, he approached the body.

He could tell immediately that it was a woman. She was slumped halfway out the window as if balancing on the edge of the windowsill.

Her heel-clad feet barely kissed the ground, and her torso was tethered to the window frame. Callan couldn't see her face, nor her hands – they were both out of the window.

But he didn't need those to know who it was. Everyone else he'd already seen tonight so it was clear – as clear as water – that Susan Knight was the dead woman.

Callan closed the door to the room behind him and led the two couples to the library. Thankfully they didn't ask any questions.

The rest of the guests – and Aileen – were waiting as per Callan's instructions in the library.

'Please wait here. All of ye.' Callan emphasised the 'all'.

'Where's Susan?' John Cook asked, looking around. His hands had left their permanent home in his pockets.

Callan assessed the group, then pierced John with a look. 'Stay here. I mean it.'

It took him fifteen more minutes to assess the corpse from outside. The window of room nine faced the other side of the inn from the library.

Just below the window, there was a small pool of blood. A flash of his torch on Susan's pale face told him the blood dripped from her forehead, but that wasn't where the injury was. There seemed to be something sparkling near her ear – almost on her neck.

He called in the forensic team and woke up Robert Davis – he needed his kit.

Knowing nothing could be done till the team arrived, he went back into the library.

John Cook was pacing, his hands back into his pockets.

They all turned as Callan came through the door, John glaring at him with barely controlled fierceness. 'Where is she?'

Callan didn't want to tell him yet. 'I cannot confirm at this point.'

But John wasn't in control. He charged headfirst at Callan.

'Sir…' Callan shut up when John fisted his hands into his shirt.

'Where's Susie?'

'Sir, please—' Callan broke off as John tried to push past him.

He wrestled the man to the ground as the dark landscape around Dachaigh was once again lit by dancing red and blue lights. His team was here.

'I'M SORRY TO INFORM YOU THAT MS KNIGHT IS DEAD.'

Aileen hated this. Of course, she'd hated murder and its brutality before, but being in such proximity to it? Knowing how the taking of a life broke down the lives of others? She shook her head. What gave someone permission to rob a person, one who was hale and hearty, of their breath?

She shuddered. It had been like a well-rehearsed play –

just like the previous time. Only it wasn't a wife who had fallen apart this time, it was a man who'd raged and collapsed, entirely defeated. And Aileen didn't know how to console him.

She'd stood stock still when others had tried to help, burst into tears of hopelessness or spurted gasps of shock.

The forensic team had arrived again, and Callan had taken over the kitchen for interviews. A few minutes later, a care officer arrived and led John Cook away.

All Aileen wanted to do was collapse onto the floor herself, but she wouldn't let panic swallow her, and she wouldn't overthink.

Aileen reminded herself to believe – in the future and her abilities.

IN THE OTHER ROOM, CALLAN STOOD WITH HIS HANDS ON the kitchen counter, listening to Martha Smith.

'Anne and I came down to discuss recipes.' Her hands trembled slightly and she sniffed back tears.

Callan waited for a beat. 'John Cook?'

'He came down a few minutes later, saying he wanted a fresh bottle of water.' After a weak shudder, she continued. 'He asked me how I was – if I was okay.'

'He doesn't seem like a considerate man—'

'Oh, what a horrid thing to say! In fact, John – Mr Cook – said he could help me sort it out. He's – he's a lawyer who helps women and I – I don't know a thing about our legal things: the investments, the mortgage and such.' Martha waved her hands. 'Dave looked after it all.'

Callan smiled a crooked smile. There had been some truth to that, he thought. Finally, Martha was being honest.

Anne Grant confirmed Martha's story.

'We didn't know what went wrong. John was with us – he asked Martha if she needed help. But then the lights went off. And we all called out to each other. And then the front door opened. We panicked…'

'And?' Callan urged her on.

Anne Grant was at least coherent this time. She held a handkerchief in her hand, which she pulled at constantly.

'John asked us to stay put when we saw the silhouette of your car out the open door. Then the lights came on and we went upstairs to check out what happened.'

The rest of the guests had been oblivious, fast asleep. They hadn't noticed that the lights were out, nor had they heard anything unusual.

'Slumbering like the beast,' Beaulieu had informed him. Richard Grant had seconded that. Their respective spouses had agreed.

When the medic called him, Callan went back to the murder scene and crouched by the body, which had now been laid out on a stretcher.

The medic nodded at him. 'Got our murder weapon.' He pointed at a thick shiny belt with studded stones on it.

'What's this?'

'Ain't an expert at this but it's a belt – an exotic sort where you pay a lot for the same functionality.'

'A jewellery piece?' Callan asked.

The medic nodded. 'Of sorts. It's the kind of thing people with a lot of money might buy. The crystals you see are diamonds. Diamonds studded on a belt!' He shook his head.

'And how did she die?'

'Strangulation. But there are no signs that she fought back. Leads me to believe I'll find something else in her system – drugs maybe. I'll send you the toxicology report'

'And the report on the previous murder?' Callan reminded him.

The medic looked down at the dead figure and let out a breath. 'Just sent it to you before you called. I had to take some time off yesterday, taking Mum to the hospital.'

Callan nodded. 'Some things are inevitable.'

The medic agreed, bagged up the body and rolled the gurney out.

Aileen intercepted Callan on his way out. She looked distraught, battling to maintain her control.

'I can't tell you much now. Tomorrow,' he promised. Lord knew she needed the night off and he needed to think.

Aileen cleared her throat. 'They said it was room nine. What was she doing there?'

'Tomorrow,' he repeated.

'They were all shocked – a killer wouldn't be shocked. And if it was anything like Dave, the murderer would have had no opportunity to clean up.'

Yes, last time there had been plenty of blood, but this was a different weapon; a different approach. Perhaps because the killer had known they had little time?

After all, what if the husband had returned to the room and found his wife gone? Though why kill the lights?

Too many questions. Callan had to sort through them soon.

'I need to write my report tonight,' he told Aileen. 'I expect to have a report on the fingerprint by tomorrow and need to read Dave's autopsy report as well. We'll discuss it all tomorrow.'

'I won't be able to sleep,' Aileen muttered. 'They might've been quarrelling but he loved her. He's broken.'

'What do you mean quarrelling?'

Aileen shook her head, looking at her feet. 'Tomorrow' she echoed.

Callan only shrugged and walked off, leaving her and the inn alone beneath the starry sky.

THE NEXT MORNING DAWNED WITH ANNOYINGLY CHEERFUL sunshine gleaming in through the windows and a throbbing headache. Aileen snorted. She must be the first Scotswoman in history to find sunshine annoying.

She had tossed and turned for hours before giving up on sleep. She'd tried to research the dagger again but felt so ill thinking about it that she'd quickly taken to pacing the room instead – and then switched on a movie when her legs had protested.

So when dawn broke the dark sky and cast its spell of a brand-new day, Aileen wasn't ready for the morning, but she went on autopilot and prepared breakfast. No one was in the mood to chat though, and the whole thing ended quickly, just like every meal since the first murder.

Aileen had asked Isla not to come over, but her loyal friend had turned up anyway, just after breakfast, and driven her to the police station. Isla's patient ear had allowed Aileen to vent, and her encouraging words – along with a chocolate chip muffin – helped Aileen feel alive again, so she walked into the station with fresh determination. She would get to the bottom of this if it was the last thing she did!

CALLAN WAS AT HIS DESK WHEN SHE ARRIVED.

'Morning.' He didn't look up.

'If you can say that.' Aileen had bags under her eyes. He'd had those too when he'd witnessed murder the first few times…

No use dwelling on the past, Cameron, Callan warned himself. Instead, he focused on the case. 'Tell me about the ring.'

Aileen's shoulders slumped. 'My grandfather gave it to my grandmother. He wasn't rich and had no money but he wanted to give her a token. So he found a stone – I think it's semi-precious – designed the ring himself and proposed.'

'Who knows about this ring?'

She considered for a moment. 'Her sons and their families – that's my mum and me. My uncle never had any children. Growing up, my father told me this story.'

'And what do you think about the ring?' Her answer would tell them whether the thief was an amateur, stealing a cheap ring by mistake, or whether he knew something they didn't.

Aileen laughed. 'That's the thing, I haven't ever seen it. And judging from the story my father told, he hasn't either.'

Callan gestured as if asking her to share more.

'Siobhan was young when my grandfather died. He was the love of her life, and it crushed her. So she moved to Loch Fuar and placed her engagement ring under lock and key. I think it reminded her of him and was too much to bear. But her wedding ring she still wears around her neck.'

Aileen lost herself in thought as Callan scratched his beard. There was something in that story, he thought.

'I have to tell you, Robert looked at the security footage, all those days and nights. It's just ye and yer guests, except Isla and yer housekeeping contractors, who enter and exit. So—'

Aileen cut Callan short. 'The murderer has to be the thief! The housekeeping contractors don't have access to my chambers. They'd need the keys for that.'

'It's best not to jump to conclusions. What we do know for sure is that it's someone who doesn't know how OCD you are about your things.'

'Hey, I am not! But you're right. Isla's the only one who knows how I am about things – that I need them in their right place at all times. I can't see how my guests – or the killer – would know that.'

But the killer knew quite a lot – like how to drug their victims.

Callan turned his laptop so she could see the screen and opened up two files.

He'd asked the teams – one from the next town, who he'd asked to help with the admin, and the other one medical – to send in their reports via email. He'd yet to print them out.

Callan had scoured the reports, updated his incident board and thought about the new information but knew he had to run it all by Aileen and get her opinions. That's what partners did, after all.

He showed her the first report and then took two long strides to the incident board.

'The autopsy report says Dave Smith never felt the dagger pierce him. He was asleep – deeply but not dead. He'd consumed pills for insomnia – Zopiclone to be exact.'

'Were they his?'

'Yes, we found the bottle. It had his and his wife's fingerprints on it. But that doesn't necessarily mean anything – she might simply have picked them up off the shelf.'

'Did you confirm with Martha that he had a prescription?'

'Yes. She told us he often suffered from insomnia.'

Aileen nodded. 'And the dose?'

'Usually one tablet an hour before bedtime, but only two or three times a week and not usually more than a couple of weeks a time,' Callan told her. 'But Dave had more than that in his system. Even if he hadn't fallen asleep yet, the medicine would have compromised his reflexes.'

'You mean to tell me someone administered the extra dosage?'

'Unless he was suicidal.'

They went back and forth, discussing the dosage, the knife and the other details of the murder.

'What about the fingerprint you lifted?'

Callan grinned. There he had had success – a key breakthrough.

'It's a match to a Percy Winston – aka Richard Grant.'

Aileen couldn't believe it. 'Why would someone from across the pond lie about their name?'

'No, he isn't from Canada – or any part of that continent. He's Percy Winston from Cheshire, England.'

'Samantha Grant? Their son – his wife? Jake Grant looks very much like Richard.'

'The connection's real enough. All four of them are from Cheshire. I'm looking into it. But guess what? They do have a business – a business that helps sell pricy vintage items.'

'Like an auctioneer?'

Callan nodded and Aileen started reading what he'd found about Percy Winston. He had two centres: one in Cheshire and another in London. The Percy Winston Gallery.

Percy pocketed a handsome commission for pricy arte-facts. And his company had indeed carried out a few auctions after an exhibition.

'You're right. He runs the company with his family. Samantha, Jake and Anne go by the same names; it's just that their surname's Winston. It sounds familiar… Wait!' Aileen clicked her fingers and strutted into the next room, back to the prehistoric computer she'd been using the day before.

She was back a few minutes later. 'The Percy Winston Gallery participated in a blind auction on the dark web. I found this name last night.' Aileen tapped a few keys on Callan's computer and brought up the page. 'I'd almost put the company at the end of my list but something held me back. They did purchase a dagger but it didn't fit the description of our murder weapon.'

Callan caught on. 'They rigged the auction?'

'No!' Aileen scrolled. 'They bought it alright, but it was a hush deal.'

She is good, Callan thought and set Aileen to work on the second murder weapon: the belt.

AILEEN RETURNED AN HOUR LATER WITH A DEFEATED LOOK on her face. The Percy Winston Gallery hadn't purchased such a belt, and their names weren't mentioned under any topic to do with the buying or selling of such an item.

'How difficult is it to find a belt studded with diamonds?'

Aileen laughed. 'Surprisingly tough as it turns out.'

With that Aileen bid him adieu. She had to get lunch ready. And her computer at home would suffice for the time being.

Isla was able to drive Aileen home before she had to get back to baking her afternoon lot.

Aileen stared out the window as the incredible Highland scenery whisked by. It looked so beautiful, so peaceful – nothing like the turmoil inside her or her inn.

Two murders at Dachaigh! Who would have thought this could ever happen? It still felt like a nightmare her subconscious refused to wake up from.

The best Aileen could do was fix her reluctant guests some sandwiches. None of them seemed to have much of an appetite, but they all picked at the sandwiches except John Cook, who'd retreated in his shell. He looked utterly heartbroken.

Legrand and Beaulieu had worried expressions on their faces. They muttered something to each other and retired to their bedroom.

Aileen checked the safe again but the ring was still gone.

Sudden flames of anger ignited her blood. How dare someone bring murder to *her* house? Dachaigh literally meant home; it was *her* home. And who would dare steal her grandmother's beloved ring? A ring made only with a semi-precious stone?

Like fuel to an engine, blood zinged through her veins, urging her to get back to her investigation.

With renewed energy, Aileen took her laptop into the kitchen and settled at the kitchen counter – the perfect place to keep an eye on things as she worked.

The 'Grants' huddled together like a pride of lions in the drawing room. Jean Beaulieu had returned downstairs while she'd been gone – Aileen saw him and Martha Smith each reading a book in the library.

Staring at her laptop, Aileen considered logistics for last night's murder first.

If a wife left the room before going to bed at night and didn't return for a while, wouldn't the husband get suspicious? She thought about John Cook. A man like that would get curious about his wife's whereabouts. But he was downstairs, alibied by two people.

She fired off a quick message to Callan.

Where did John think Susan was? She went to the other room. Wouldn't he get suspicious?

WHEN NO RESPONSE CAME, AILEEN ROLLED HER EYES. Callan used technology like an old man; he considered gadgets his enemy.

She set to work on the belt again. There were several such studded belts in production so it wasn't a one-off piece unless Callan had missed something, although they certainly weren't sold in as many numbers as the normal belts everyday mortals wore.

After what felt like ages, Aileen rubbed her tired eyes and checked the clock. It was mid-afternoon already. She'd been running around in circles with that blasted belt, like a hamster on a wheel, heading nowhere.

Raking her mind, she thought about her first trip to the station after the murder and recalled seeing Richard Grant, aka Percy Winston, with Jean Beaulieu. She'd forgotten to mention it to Callan.

She reassessed the scene in her mind. They'd appeared to be in a deep serious conversation, but based on the security footage she'd checked, they'd left the inn at different times and returned separately, again at different times.

A chance run-in? Her gut doubted it.

Aileen drummed her fingers on her desk, thinking, before her phone rang, jolting her back to reality.

Callan's voice boomed down the line. 'Can Siobhan take visitors?'

'Do you want to meet her?' Aileen didn't want to imagine the disappointment in her grandmother's face when she told her about the recent disastrous events at Dachaigh.

Aileen had failed her grandmother – failed as guardian of the inn her grandmother had built from nothing.

'She'd be the best candidate to tell us information about the ring.'

Aileen knew he was right and called her grandmother as soon as he rang off. She only hoped Siobhan would forgive her when she found out what was going on.

Thankfully, Siobhan's nurse picked up, giving her a brief stay of execution.

'Siobhan's napping. She spends half the night hooked on to the TV like she doesn't need her sleep, and I know she's been knocking back a few fingers of whisky whenever she gets the chance,' Nancy, the nurse, whispered the last part.

Aileen had to laugh at that. She had no doubt Siobhan had made a resourceful friend – someone who could smuggle her whisky in regularly. Her gran was a rebel that way.

Without drawing out her luck or risking her grand-mother waking up, she set up an appointment to visit the next day.

They'd find out what Siobhan had to say about all this.

CHAPTER TWELVE

T he rest of the day passed without a hitch. Going to bed that night, Aileen hoped there wouldn't be any new surprises.

Her car had been towed by the mechanic, but it would take at least a week for her new tyres to be delivered to Loch Fuar; they weren't the sort the garage kept in stock. Despite that small annoying detail, Aileen assured herself the night would be a peaceful one. Peace meant no thieves, false alarms or murders, she specified, if luck was listening.

Everyone felt on alert, and even her obscure guests seemed to be keeping an eye out for suspicious activities.

With that knowledge, Aileen shut her eyes and willed for sleep.

She got what she wanted, because the next time she opened her eyes, it was daylight.

Unlike her content smile, the day didn't share her optimism. Compared to the previous few days, the sun had suddenly turned shy, hiding behind thick grey clouds.

Isla turned up with fresh bread and helped fry eggs and

bacon for breakfast. Aileen stirred savoury baked beans on the stove. 'I hope Gran's fine.'

Isla laughed. 'She's as healthy as a horse! The only reason she stays in that place is because of the luxury of having someone at her beck and call.'

Aileen agreed. 'She is *ninety!* Staying so far away in a small town with limited medical facilities isn't the best choice for her.'

Isla winked. 'Age is just a number.'

It was surprising to see all her guests at the breakfast table. The air was still solemn, as it had been for all meals. Well, except for the one happy dinner they'd shared the night before the first murder. That joyful pretence had been shattered like a thin plane of glass.

John Cook had heavy pouches under his eyes, eyes that looked hollow. They hadn't been overly expressive before, beyond their vigilant gaze, but now they were just a deep abyss with no substance.

The so-called 'Grants' sat quietly, too. Jake rubbed circles on his wife's back, avoiding eye contact with his parents, but Samantha and Richard did not attempt a conversation.

Louis Legrand strode in and surveyed the assembled guests. He gave them all a hard look and took a seat as far from them as he could.

Jean Beaulieu followed on his heels, his stubby face downcast.

Martha Smith was the last to make an appearance, but she looked better than she had the last couple of days, although the laughter in her eyes and the skip in her step had long deserted her.

One of them was a murderer, Aileen thought. And a thief.

Who could it be?

The clock chiming the hour pulled Aileen from her deep thoughts.

She cleaned up the kitchen and got down to the rest of her innkeeper duties.

A while later, Legrand walked up to her, hands in his pockets.

After a brief assessment of the kitchen, he seemed to look at Aileen down his nose. He took a superior poise that sharpened his chiselled features.

'Jean and I don't want anyone to clean our rooms.'

'So the *Do Not Disturb* card on your door says.'

'Just clarifying.'

Aileen hadn't entered their room since the couple had shown up. The cleaning crew hadn't entered either. Aileen had guessed their need for privacy was far greater than their need for clean sheets.

Thinking of housekeeping, Aileen thought about the other rooms. She had a service do the cleaning for her – maybe she could ask them if they'd found anything suspicious.

Later, when Aileen spoke her thoughts aloud to Callan, he told her not to bother. They were on their way to see Siobhan. Callan had insisted he drive there instead of taking the rare train into town.

'Already asked the cleaning company. They found nothing out of the ordinary. And they say room two has a perpetual DND on their door.'

'Aye, that's the couple who trades in jewellery.'

Callan nodded. 'Ah yes. Do you only lodge adults? You've got no family staying with young children.'

Aileen waved her hands. 'Nothing like that. The current guests booked via the new website.'

'No one cancelled?'

'No.'

'So all your ten guests randomly booked their accommodation. And are you sure they've never met each other?'

'As far as I know, they're all strangers. Except for their spouses, that is.' Aileen pointed at Callan, 'The Grants are a family.'

Callan nodded, 'I had considered that. None of your guests are staying alone and the killings looked to be a single person's job, as far as the death blow was concerned. Would a spouse know?'

Callan caressed his scruff before continuing, 'Did you find anything out about the belt?'

Aileen huffed out a breath. 'Only that too many people have idle cash to buy diamond-studded belts they'll probably hide behind their shirts.'

Callan cracked up at that. He seemed to be in an unusually good mood.

'What did Susan tell John that he didn't think it was unusual for his wife to leave their room?' Aileen asked.

'She told him she was going to the library. So he told me.'

That was a plausible explanation. The inn's library stood away from the kitchen and drawing room. So when John came down that night, he wouldn't have seen her, and he'd only have known she wasn't there if he'd purposefully gone to check.

Callan continued with his explanation. 'She did that often, according to Mr Cook. Ms Knight loved to read. Apparently, she'd been reading a mystery and was eager to know whodunnit.'

They both fell into silence as Callan's rugged car sped across the Highland landscape. There were almost no other cars on the road.

Tall, ancient mountains lined either side of the winding road. Loch Fuar peeked out from behind the mountains and then disappeared as they left the loch behind.

A stream ran with them before parting ways a short while later.

The blue sky had disappeared as if signalling something disastrous was approaching. Aileen hoped it wasn't a storm. She didn't want to get stuck in the middle of nowhere.

'Why'd ye leave the big town then?' Callan's gruff voice shattered the silence.

'Huh?' Aileen took a while to catch on. 'It's quite the story.'

Almost an embarrassing one, Aileen knew.

'We have a while to drive yet. And it's interesting. Ye had a good job,' Callan pushed.

Aileen considered his remark. She'd known Callan had looked her up. Besides, a partial truth wouldn't hurt.

She cleared her throat. 'Well, it was a big city, as you said. I spent almost a decade there but wasn't satisfied with life.'

Callan waited for her to continue.

'Too many people, too many cars, noise, pollution and the cost of living. I thought it would be a good idea to leave it all behind and come to Loch Fuar.'

'Come to Loch Fuar to run an inn?' Callan enquired. He was egging her on, a dash of disbelief in his voice.

Aileen looked over at the inspector. His face was drawn in a concentrated frown but he wasn't solely focused on the road. He was trying to get gossip out of her.

And as a trained interrogator, he would do a good job. He'd catch her lies as easily as a consummate fisherman pulled fish from his inescapable net.

'Yeah, Loch Fuar's a nice place. I enjoyed my summers here as a child, helping Gran.'

'Heard you were as good as any... What's it called... Forensic accountant. Siobhan told everyone how you slaved for those stiff backs just to make partner.'

Aileen pressed her lips together. 'It was something I was working towards, but then I didn't want that anymore.'

Callan smirked as if he knew she was lying, but he didn't push her any further − he just took a deep breath and changed the subject.

DESPITE HER AGE, SIOBHAN'S CAT-LIKE BLUE EYES WERE still sharp. She also had a strong sixth sense, which meant they couldn't even consider hiding details from her.

Besides, it was obvious they had a rat in their midst.

Rory MacDonald, Callan mused. It wasn't hard to guess − his boss and Siobhan had always had their heads pressed together when it came to the town gossip. Callan smiled to himself, promising he'd make sure Rory paid for his treachery, boss or not.

Siobhan assessed the two young people in front of her as she sat in her armchair. But the armchair and the hospital tape around her wrist was all a ruse. If the time came, she'd be able to do a handstand as easily as any young man or woman.

Her voice never quivered with age, nor did her wit.

She pointed a finger at Aileen. 'She's healthy, and so are you.' She pressed a look towards Callan. 'Didn't you consider asking my granddaughter out?'

'Gran!' Aileen squeaked in shock.

Callan laughed and shook his head.

'You aren't buried six feet under, nor have you creaking bones. Young flesh and blood! Whatever are ye waiting for?' Siobhan said, exaggerating every word with frivolous hand gestures.

'Gran, that's enough.' Aileen tried a firm voice.

Siobhan scoffed. 'Lookie here. Ma grandwean's trying to teach me manners. Hah!' She slapped wrinkled yet strong hands on the arm of her chair.

Directing her gaze at Callan, she negotiated, 'Ask her out and I'll tell ye about the ring.'

Callan grinned a boyish grin. Siobhan didn't believe in beating about the bush. Raising two young boys had given her a firm hand and a very good knack for negotiation.

He didn't argue. 'Aye, I'll do that but you tell us first.'

She gave them another look. 'I like a good blether. And I like how you don't beat about the bush.'

She took a breath and launched into a speech.

'I lied.' She looked at Aileen first. 'It wasn't a fake ring. A man wouldn't notice the difference, real or fake. But I, like most women, know a real stone when I see one.'

'You never showed the ring to anyone!' Aileen pointed out.

Siobhan cracked a laugh. 'They never asked. I had to make a sob story about missing ma Eddie.' The old lady sighed then. 'With the ring or without, I miss him every breath I take.'

Siobhan latched a hand onto the golden chain around her neck. She pulled it out to show a golden band hanging from it.

This time she looked at Callan. 'We never have enough time with the ones we love the most. There's no time to waste. And you must enjoy every moment. You'll know what I'm talking about.'

For a while, Siobhan gazed out of the window, as if she was remembering her youthful days with Eddie.

'Edward Mackinnon was as handsome a man as I'd

ever met. My ma warned me against him. I didn't listen. Since I was the baby of the family, the last of five, I felt they controlled me too much.'

Siobhan waved a hand. 'Eddie, he wasn't a gentle sort of man; he was a thief.'

Siobhan's firm words made Aileen gasp in shock.

'Don't look so horrified, dearie. I loved him for that. Why, we played the field together for a while before I had our first bairn.'

Siobhan's sly smile suggested this strong yet gentle old woman had caused plenty of trouble in her youth, and her old eyes glittered with mirth.

'Louis XIV's diamonds, that's what we called them. They were being sent out of his court to someone in England. A secret deal of sorts. The poor messenger made it to the coast, then got accosted.' Siobhan laughed. 'We think he survived, but the pouch of diamonds was gone.'

Aileen leaned forward in her chair, a stunned look on her face. Callan suppressed a smile.

'Eddie was after them when we met. I joined him on his quest. We were in love and we were young – reckless.

'He had his ears to the ground and when we had enough information, we took them from under a jeweller's nose. It was more romantic than a movie.'

A dizzy look came over Siobhan's face, and she smiled a sweet smile, reminiscing about the old times.

Finally, she nodded at the present. 'He designed the ring for me, from one of those diamonds. Nothing too huge – that wouldn't have suited my fingers.' She held out her thin but steady hand.

'We sold the rest. Gave up that life once we knew the bairn was on its way. We couldn't risk it after that.'

Aileen cleared her throat. 'Why lie about the ring being fake then?'

Her grandmother smirked. 'If we'd told the truth, your father would have been taken away to another family and I'd have rotted away in prison.'

Siobhan continued. 'We told everyone the ring was made using a semi-precious stone. And I hardly ever wore it out for people to see. When Eddie was gone, I brought the boys to Loch Fuar and hid the ring, spinning a tale of how it reminded me of my late husband.'

She laughed a sarcastic laugh. 'Locking a ring away could never separate my thoughts from Eddie.'

With that, Siobhan caressed her wedding ring with such love it felt too intimate to witness.

'SIOBHAN'S SOMETHING!' CALLAN SAID, SMILING AT THE thought of the old woman's youthful law-breaking.

Aileen huffed out a breath as they drove back to Loch Fuar. 'My father would have a coronary! He's a criminal lawyer, for God's sake!'

At that admission, Callan drowned the car in fits of belly-hurting laughter.

When his amusement finally subsided, he snorted out, 'Siobhan would have had a good laugh at the exemplary vocation one of her sons had taken up.'

Aileen pressed her lips together; she refused to comment on what her uncle did for a living. She couldn't let Callan enjoy another laugh at her family's expense.

Wanting to distract him, she turned the conversation to important matters. 'So the ring's a real one. That changes things.'

Callan dropped his shoulders, his eyes trained on the road. 'I expect the autopsy as well as the tox report for the second murder soon.'

'We know someone strangled her.'

'Aye, but there seems to be no violence, no signs of a struggle.'

She nodded. Aileen knew if someone tried to choke her, her body would fight back.

A thought came to her mind. 'What about the sleeping pills?'

'Unless someone has a second bottle… We took the first one in evidence. It was right next to Smith's bed – on the table.'

Aileen breathed in a shaky breath. Talking about the bed made her feel queasy. She knew she could never sleep in a bed where someone had been killed. Besides, the mattress was a done deal – the knife had cut through it.

She took a deep breath. The room was still locked under the police tape, but Aileen knew she would need to revamp it… Again. She couldn't very well have guests arriving to a room full of bloodstains.

That was if she had any new customers in the future. However depressing the thought was, it was true. How many cancellations had poured in since the first murder?

Aileen shook herself. All it meant was that she'd just have to work harder with Callan to get to the bottom of this.

Callan drove them to the police station and parked hastily.

Aileen left him to work on her computer at the inn, muttering about belts.

Fuelling up with a cup of coffee, Callan checked his email and found the reports.

He sat —the coffee going cold at his elbow— reading the autopsy and toxicology report of Susan Knight.

There was no doubt she'd died from the lack of oxygen supply.

Ah, here was the twist…

The killer —based on what the report read— had to have been at least as tall as Susan, if not more. That meant Beaulieu was out of the question. Callan remembered the short Frenchman had barely reached up to Susan's eyes when they'd all stood in the library after Dave Smith's murder.

But what Callan found interesting was the blood he'd seen dripping from Susan's forehead to the ground below.

They were just a few drops, but one of the diamonds in the belt had pricked her neck, drawing some blood.

Callan stroked his chin.

But again there were no other marks on the body. She'd scraped at her throat but put up no real fight.

Another dose of that darned sleeping drug.

The tox report confirmed she had injected Zopiclone in her system. But, Callan mused, not as much as Dave.

So the killer led her into that room and Susan went willingly.

But what was she doing when the killer wrapped that belt around her neck? Perhaps she was too incapacitated to react, already too drowsy to know…

It would certainly have been risky, given that the door wasn't locked. And John could've gone to the library to meet with his partner.

The killer would need to be careful. He'd have to have dosed Susan at least an hour before he'd killed her. But how could he have administered the drug? Some sort of ruse… But what?

He needed to talk to John Cook again.

Nodding to himself, Callan stood. Another visit to Dachaigh was in order, home to two murder scenes. And he wanted some answers…

As Callan raced through the peaceful Highlands, his email chimed. It was an email from the other inspector – the one from the next town he'd asked to help with the admin side of things. He'd been looking into the missing ring.

Once at Dachaigh, Callan quickly pulled open the email and frowned. It was a detailed financial synopsis on Susan Knight's bank account.

Perhaps they'd find some connection to Dave Smith in there.

Oh well, Callan was at the inn, perhaps he could ask Aileen to interpret the records for him.

He found Aileen frowning at the laptop screen she'd set up in her kitchen.

'Susan's financial records. What can you tell me?'

Pursing her lips, Aileen gave him a stern look. Wordlessly, she scanned the numbers.

After a moment, Aileen said, 'That she was brilliant at her job and got paid for it…Susan wasn't wanting for money.'

Callan watched Aileen bite her lips, something she'd never done before… He cleared his throat.

'Anything else that could tell us why she was murdered?'

Aileen shook her head, 'I'll need some time to get through this. At first glance, I can tell her financial records are separate from that of John's. It's not usual nor is it unheard off.'

'Could they have a separate joint account?'

Aileen nodded slowly, 'It's quite possible. You can ask

John about it or I can find it out for you. If they had a joint account, she would have withdrawn or deposited cash in there.'

Slipping hands in his pocket, Callan said, 'Right. As soon as you find out, let me know.'

Aileen was already hacking away at the numbers. She didn't respond.

JOHN COOK WASN'T HAPPY TO SEE HIM.

'I had some questions.'

'Just find whoever did this. Just…' John rubbed his tired eyes.

'Did you have a bank account together with Ms Knight?'

John cast a withering look. 'Money! You think I did that to her for her money?'

'It's just a question Mr Cook. I'm not implying anything. Did you have a joint bank account?'

Cook shook his head. 'Go away.'

Callan pushed through. 'Did she drink water before bed the night she… Died?'

'Water? I…' John waved his hands in a vague gesture. 'Maybe.'

'Ye don't know her night routine? Most women have a routine they follow diligently every night.' At John's confused look Callan added, 'So my sister tells me.'

'You aren't making sense, Inspector… Susan would often read at night. I usually fell asleep before her.'

'But you didn't the night Dave Smith was killed.'

That got him. John stood, showing signs of agitation. He pointed a finger at Callan and spoke between clenched teeth, 'Look here! I loved her and now she's gone.

Someone killed her! Susan, who always stood for the truth!'

He shuddered out a breath.

'She was tired that night. There was a presentation she was working on; she'd barely slept the last few nights. This was supposed to be a trip for us to unwind. We both have busy schedules.'

John paused and ran a hand through his hair. 'Had. It's all in the past now.'

'Did she consume water the night she died?' Callan asked again.

John shook his head. 'Not when I was there, but she went to the library for an hour or so – said she wanted to finish her book. Susan never likes it when— um, liked it when someone disturbed her. She'd be too engrossed in her book, but I should've checked up on her. I should've checked.' John sank into a chair.

Callan left the grieving widower alone and returned to the station, where he found Aileen pacing his office.

'What-'

She didn't give him a chance to speak. 'I needed to access some files so I hitched a ride into town. Rory helped-'

Taking a breath, Callan sat at his desk.

Aileen said, 'So, I looked into the belt again but I'm just running into walls. We need another angle. What did the autopsy say?'

She almost vibrated — ruffled, restless. The first thing Callan knew when it came to murder was that it needed patience: committing one as well as solving one. So he brewed her a cup of coffee, settled her in his uncomfortable visitor's chair and led her through the report he'd received. To save time, he entered the new details onto his incident board as he went.

'She was strangled with the belt – had to be in that same room; too suspicious otherwise – but dosed with Zopiclone before she was called to the room. That's the unclear part – how the Zopiclone entered her system. Knight never suspected it, and she was too drowsy to fight back. So there was no real tussle or any cry for help to alert anyone.'

'Yes, I agree – it had to be in that room.'

'And the medicine would have had to be working, placing it about an hour after it was administered, otherwise the guests in the neighbouring rooms would've heard.'

Callan and Aileen exchanged a glance, then Aileen shivered. He didn't blame her. Cold-blooded murder where the victims didn't even realise their end had come was a cold, cold thing.

He wondered if it was personal vengeance or if it was impersonal? Purely professional?

Aileen squared her shoulders then. 'Susan had a very complex looking bank account. There are several deposits, large sums too. However, I'm looking into Percy Winston and Jean Beaulieu for now.'

She proceeded to tell him about seeing them together at Barbara's tea shop. Callan paced while he listened.

'Beaulieu's married to a jeweller and knows enough about the business. Maybe you need to dig into his deals to find that belt.'

Aileen huffed. 'I ran a full check on him as well as Louis Legrand. As far as I can see, they haven't made such a deal before.'

'Check again. As well as Susan's finances.'

Aileen simply stood up and walked out.

BACK IN THE OTHER ROOM, SHE PLOPPED ON THE CHAIR opposite to the computer and reran her search, going through all their past deals, but she came up empty-handed... Again.

Perhaps she ought to look at what they were up to currently.

Aileen began to leaf through data, some hidden in the dark and some in the light.

It was only when the closet-like room began to get on her nerves that she resurfaced. Another fifteen minutes and her reddened eyes would pop out of their sockets.

Besides, she'd dug very deep. If only she could pin Percy Winston's name to a lucrative deal for the diamond belt, Callan could have a strong case against the man.

Aileen stepped out of the police station and breathed in the fresh Highland air. It had drizzled while she'd been cooped up inside. The road was wet, and the air smelled of damp earth, though weak yet hopeful rays of sun splashed mirth on her face.

Aileen stood there for a while, soaking in the sun's welcoming warmth. It was so peaceful here – no brutal engine noise shattering nature's song or unnecessary honking that splintered human ears. Nor were there too many people crowding you out.

The town centre around the corner might be the busiest place in Loch Fuar but the street that the police station stood on was quiet.

One old couple walked towards the market square with a trolley tagging behind them. The wheels rattled on the uneven footpath.

A handful of cars were parked on the opposite side of the road. This side was reserved for police vehicles. Though thinking about the three-person team of the Loch

Fuar police, it was a wonder they had a police vehicle at all.

The door behind her pushed open and Rory Macdonald walked out.

'Lovely day.'

'Aye,' Aileen agreed as they both stood taking in their surroundings.

Rory stuffed his hands in his pockets and stood with his legs shoulder-width apart. 'Thought about leaving this behind once for the big city. I was a lad looking for big things in life.'

'Oh?' Aileen had learned by now that when someone started talking about themselves in this town, it was the listener's duty to urge them on.

The old man nodded. 'A week was enough for me to realise I was a small-town lad at heart and always will be. I missed joking with the old grandfathers who'd gather in the pub to share a hearty laugh over whisky.'

He compressed his lips together. 'Best decision I ever made.' Rory nodded at Aileen. 'On that note, I'll go join the crowd, considering I'm a grandpa myself now.'

'Congratulations!'

Rory simply waved his hands. 'Grandwean number three is on her way soon. I've got to entertain the other two tonight.'

And with a happy smile, he walked away.

Aileen's face had also turned into an involuntary smile. Coming to Loch Fuar had been a good choice for her too, as long as the murderer was caught.

On that note, she turned like a soldier during a drill and paraded inside. It was time to renew her efforts.

Callan was looking into the diamond ring. What was its significance?

He paced as he looked at his board and pondered. If the killer was after the ring, he or she surely would've attacked Aileen, not the other two. Why kill if the murderer already had the ring?

It didn't add up; the ring and the murders. Were they unrelated? Just a bad coincidence?

His feet clomped as he walked back and forth in a rhythm that would have irritated another person.

Hell! It just didn't add up.

The old case files on the diamonds were obscure as well. The inspector working on them had been nowhere close to the real thieves. No trail led to either Siobhan or Edward Mackinnon. And there was no mention of the diamonds they'd managed to sell either.

Callan's gut told him the ring was still in the inn. There had been little opportunity to smuggle it out, and Robert Davis had had an eye out for anyone leaving Loch Fuar or anyone new coming in.

He thought about the sleeping drug. The killer clearly knew about it, and how to administer it. And he or she had access to it. But then the information on Zopiclone was easy enough to find online.

His stomach let out a rebellious growl. Callan muttered a curse and glanced at his wristwatch. He had forgotten about lunch!

Armed with two huge sandwiches and warm cappuccinos Callan walked into the small room Aileen sat in.

Was she dozing off?

No, he realised, that was just how she worked – her shoulders slouched in front of the computer screen, her normally neat hair disturbed by her restless hands and her fingers drumming a tune of their own on the desk.

Callan smirked, tiptoed to the desk and with more force than necessary dropped the bag bursting with their lunch sandwiches beside her.

Aileen yelped at the sudden movement and put a hand on her heart as if to hold it in place before she turned to him. Despite her clear efforts to put on a poker face, her mortification shone through.

Callan gave her a mocking smirk, but before she could lose her temper at him, he placed a steaming coffee cup in her hand.

'You're welcome.' He raised his cup in a toast. 'Have you found anything?'

Aileen set her cup down and rubbed her tired eyes.

'I looked at Jean Beaulieu again. I focused on the deals he's currently handling for their company.'

She turned to the computer and pulled open a file.

'I did some hacking.'

Callan raised a surprised eyebrow. It took some guts to hack into another computer while sitting in a police station.

Aileen tilted her head. 'It took me some time to get into their files. I must say: the killer could also have used this data to steal the belt. He or she would know they had it in their possession. Careful as Legrand and Beaulieu are, they've their files on the cloud. And they connected their gadgets to my Wi-Fi.'

Based on her smirk, Callan thought it was best not to know how exactly she'd got into those files.

Pointing a finger to his warrant card, he said, 'Not the best thing to divulge to an officer of the law.'

She shrugged as if she didn't care.

These Mackinnon women were something else, Callan mused; one hustled diamonds and the other was a part-time hacker!

'It's basic and all for a good cause. No need for you to write it up in your report.'

'And how would I get the evidence for court?'

'An anonymous tip perhaps. Or if you're any good at interviewing, they'll tell you.'

'I'm good at those,' Callan muttered indignantly.

Aileen smirked at him looking entirely too pleased with herself. 'Or you could simply ask Charles Wyatt about the belt.'

'Who's that?'

She pointed at something on the screen. 'Legrand and Beaulieu aren't here on a vacation. And that's perhaps why they've kept everyone out of their room for so many days. They're here to do business with a man called Charles Wyatt.'

Aileen continued, 'According to your records, he lives on the Isle of Skye and owns a cottage a few miles from here.'

Callan didn't ask her how she'd accessed police records. Thinking about it now, he didn't want to know how she'd found most of the information about the dagger either.

He nodded at Aileen. 'That's good information; since the belt's got nothing to do with Percy Winston, aka Richard Grant, I'm bringing him in for an interview. At least I'll find out about the dagger.'

Callan turned and walked towards the door, only to stop when Aileen cleared her throat.

'You shouldn't raise suspicion. If Beaulieu catches your scent, he might destroy evidence.'

Callan squinted at her, stroking his chin.

'It's just a follow-up interview. No need for anyone to know about the fingerprint I lifted.'

With that, Callan left for Dachaigh.

It was a cakewalk to get Richard Grant into the Interview Room. Either he thought he could play Callan or he assumed the police weren't smart enough to get to the bottom of things.

Callan had walked into the inn's drawing room to find him sitting by the window, looking out.

John Cook sat in the other chair, deep in thought.

'Mr Grant,' he began. 'I have some questions regarding…' Callan cleared his throat and looked at John.

Richard nodded and stood. Callan walked out to his car and Richard followed.

'You were in the next room, so I have a few questions. But they're a little sensitive and I'd hate for anyone to overhear. Would you mind coming into the police station?'

'Am I under suspicion, Inspector?'

'Have you done anything I should be suspicious of?' Callan laughed a friendly sort of laugh. He was good at play-acting. 'It'll help me solve the murders quicker.'

Richard shrugged. 'Anything that'll help us see the back of this unpleasant business.'

So just like that Callan got Richard Grant into an interview room.

'So, the night of the first murder, did you hear anything unusual?'

'No, we were jet-lagged.' Richard rolled his Rs, speaking in a Canadian accent.

'Right.' Callan nodded. 'And the second murder?'

'I was feeling a bit under the weather. Sam brought a tray upstairs for me; I ate it and retired to bed.'

'So you heard nothing?'

'Not until you banged on our door.'

Callan changed the topic. 'What is it that you do for a living?'

'We have a gallery. It has some space for temporary exhibitions.'

'Ever seen a dagger like this one?' Callan showed him the picture of the murder weapon used to kill Dave Smith.

Cynical eyes appraised him. 'I organise exhibitions, not museum pieces, Inspector.'

'That's not what the record says about you, Percy.'

Richard's expression turned from cynical to surprised for a single heartbeat, then he quickly turned it into an impatient one.

'Richard – my name's Richard.'

Callan flashed a sinister smile. 'Richard.' He snorted. 'Percy Winston suits you better.'

'You've lost your mind. I don't know who you're talking about.'

'You bought this dagger, didn't you?' Callan spoke as if he hadn't heard him.

Richard sat back in his chair. He kept his fury in check, instead of showing an air of confusion. 'You aren't making sense. I'm calling my lawyer.'

'Where's your lawyer from, Percy Winston?'

Slamming both his beefy hands on the table, Richard stood. 'That's not my name.'

'Oh, but it is.' Callan was enjoying this. 'Why, that's who owns this dagger. The dagger that pierced Dave Smith's heart and took his life. That robbed a woman of her husband.'

Like a toddler throwing a tantrum, Richard Grant, aka Percy Winston, banged the table again. This time his disdain and anger oozed from every pore. He clenched his teeth and spoke every syllable clearly. 'I didn't kill him.'

Callan called his bluff.

To that all Percy Winston said was, 'Lawyer.'

CHAPTER THIRTEEN

Aileen paced the closet-like room.

Callan walked in. 'Screamed lawyer but my gut tells me he's speaking the truth.'

'You didn't figure out what he was threatening someone about?'

He shook his head.

'It was after the murder and the other voice I heard was male.' Callan began to pace as well.

'Could it be Jake?' Aileen asked.

Callan scratched his scruff and nodded. 'Aye, I think so, and I think they were arguing about the dagger. But Percy threatened his son. He threatened to go to the police – said he knew what Jake had done.'

Aileen understood perfectly what Callan was saying. 'But we can't place Jake at the murder scene nor in the room where Percy threatened him. And Percy isn't talking.'

Callan nodded. 'I hope his lawyer's level-headed and cooperative. But I can't wrap my head around this. I heard the other voice say he'd sold it.'

'A good lawyer will weave him out of this mess. We'll just have to see what Percy says, especially about his son.'

'Aye, a decent lawyer could get him out. We just don't have enough evidence.'

Aileen hummed and stared at the wall behind Callan. It was as plain as Callan's all-black attire.

'Callan, what do you think about the dagger?'

'That it killed that twat, Dave Smith.'

Aileen waved her hands, 'I mean, we traced it to Percy Winston, didn't we? But could a murderer use such a… Differentiable murder weapon and leave it behind for the police to find?'

Callan shrugged, 'Either he is idiotic or cocky. It could be his downfall.'

'Somehow, I doubt that…'

Thudding the coffee mug on his desk, Callan turned to the laptop. 'I heard the other voice say they sold it.'

Aileen clarified, 'I didn't find any such transaction.'

Callan pointed at his computer screen, 'My colleague just emailed this to me. An anonymous bidder purchased the same dagger almost a month ago…'

'So Percy Winston-'

'Could either have set up the ruse of selling it or could truly have sold it.'

CALLAN AND AILEEN BOTH SAT IN THAT CRAMPED OFFICE and tried to make sense of the situation.

Callan stared at his incident board. 'Tell me, what do you know about Samantha Grant and Susan Knight?'

Aileen raised a questioning eyebrow but answered nonetheless, 'They are both guests at my inn. Personable ladies, I must say.'

'Have ye seen them together— in a friendly sort of way, I mean?'

Drumming her fingers on Callan's overcrowded desk, Aileen said, 'Can't say I have. Susan never came down for dinner the night Dave was murdered. And apart from when all of us had gathered, they haven't been together. Why do you ask?'

Callan began to pace, as he reported what he'd seen the day Aileen's tyres were slashed. 'I wonder what they were doing standing there?'

Aileen cleared her throat, 'Was that the last time you saw Susan alive?'

Was that emotion he heard in Aileen's voice?

'Yes, I think so. And that got me thinking…' Callan suddenly trailed off.

'What?' Aileen urged him.

'Coincidence.'

'Aye, it's too much of a coincidence that the lights went out that same night as Susan was killed.'

Callan plopped down on his uncomfortable chair, trying his best to hide the grimace of pain.

'It could've been a local vendor irked by your return. But as you said, it wasn't just the car tyres but also the blackout, your gran's ring going missing and the murder. Coincidence? That's bollocks! So what's the link between all these?'

Aileen nodded, 'There has to be some significance.'

Callan plopped his hands on his desk and saw Aileen grimace at the piles of crumpled papers littering his desk.

'Ye're a snob.'

Aileen sat back, derailed by that comment, 'Excuse me?'

'You just wrinkled yer nose at my desk-'

'Because it's disgusting.'

Callan smirked. 'I'm a very busy man. After all, I'm the one cleaning up the mess ye created.'

'Me? What did I do?'

'Revamped the inn and invited guests in without so much as checking their identities. And yer pathetic security-'

Aileen slammed her hands on his desk. 'I never asked for this! Besides you file like a five-year-old-'

'You fight like a toddler.'

'Stuffing crumpled papers into a folder.'

Callan cackled with amusement.

'Oh God, Aileen, it's such fun arguing with ye! It doesn't take long to get ye riled up!'

Aileen brandished her teeth at him. 'You don't rile me up.' She muttered defiantly before turning her attention towards her laptop screen.

His amusement settled, Callan went back to the evening before Susan Knight's murder.

'You were out the entire day. And Susan, as I said, was alive and breathing. The only reason someone would want ye to get "hung up" would be the thief.'

Her voice a little piqued, Aileen said, 'You think they stole Gran's ring?'

Callan pointed a finger, 'You couldn't have driven back to Dachaigh, even if ye were at that vendor meeting. Ye'd be late and that's plenty of time to locate the safe and steal the ring.

'Golly,' Aileen muttered. 'Could Samantha and Susan have slashed my car tyres?'

'They saw me and walked away... You know what bugs me?' Callan spoke as if to himself. 'None of them heard the sounds ye did that night Dave was killed.'

'Well, they would all be asleep? What's that got to do with my car?'

'Asleep? Bah Humbug! I think they were all expecting those footsteps! And that's the crux of this puzzle.'

AILEEN WALKED INTO CALLAN'S CRAMPED OFFICE WITH A steaming coffee pot, her head churning.

'My keys,' she began with no preamble. 'Why were they picked twice?'

Clearly in a rough mood, Callan looked at Aileen through tired eyes. He reached towards his right knee, unconsciously massaging it.

'What are yer theories?'

Huffing, Aileen plopped in the visitor's chair. 'I could only come up with one: the person who wanted to copy them got something wrong and needed the keys again.'

Callan rubbed his eyes. 'Plausible except, it was two different people who must have done this.'

'I can't believe two of my guests are crooks!'

The vicious smile on Callan's face made Aileen shiver, 'The second one seems to be more cautious. He or she at least returned the keys back to yer pocket.'

'Do you think that is significant?'

'To be honest, yer keys are a means to commit the crime. It can be a possible explanation of how the killer got into Dave's room that night.'

Aileen shook herself. 'The fault of having old lock and key doors.'

Callan snorted. 'Hotel keycards are a mess! But aye, if Dave had locked the door the killer could have easily unlocked it.'

'I don't understand this man, Dave Smith. I mean, who is he?'

Callan only shrugged, placing a sheet of paper in front of Aileen.

'My admin contacted the police in Edinburgh. We just got this email from them.'

Aileen gasped. They'd found the man she'd known as Dave Smith.

Callan's cocky smirk lifted some of the tiredness from his eyes, 'This inspector has been looking for our man for a few months now. Our killer got Dave good. Dave Smith-'

'Was a black-market dealer—a con man…' Aileen lost her words as she went through the list of identities Dave Smith had taken on.

Finally, she put the printed email down and said, 'Good Lord! That man changed identities like clothes.'

Callan made a tsk sound. 'He did. And so obviously did his wife. But that doesn't explain what I saw.'

Raising a questioning eyebrow, Aileen asked, 'What did you see?'

'I saw the two of them, early one morning by the lochside. And it had to be them, it corroborates with Martha's mood and Dave's disappearance that entire day.'

'What could they be doing there? Are you sure it was them?'

Callan shrugged, 'Beats me…Although I can tell ye it ain't one of the locals. So it's got to be one of yer guests.'

Pacing with his hands in his pocket, Callan continued, 'Martha Smith is the only one with that wild hair. I saw the hair, and I didn't know who it could be then. But Dave and Martha were fighting.'

'Oh, God! Oh, God!' Aileen said pulling her hair and sank into the chair a bit more. 'I know now where I saw that! Dave and Martha; when he came down for dinner the night before his death—I saw Martha flinch as if she were scared of her husband.'

Callan smacked the desk. 'Damn it! She couldn't have done it.'

'Her alibi's strong for the second murder-'

'There's no vengeance.'

Aileen raised a questioning eyebrow before standing to pour herself another cup of coffee. She needed something strong to keep her brain from exploding.

Callan breathed in the bitter fragrance, savouring it for a moment.

'Dave Smith's killing blow, delivered at around three in the morning was a simple kill. The killer knew he wouldn't move; he'd overdosed on sleeping pills. It's a cold-blooded murder. Now Martha— being the wife and an abused one at that— would want to rage at her husband. But we have one killing blow, no combat wounds.'

'So the sleeping pills: what's their significance?'

'Aye, the sleeping pills - our killer's a coward. He or she doesn't want their victims to hold up a fight. Besides, it's risky in an inn full of people. But a simple overdose is boring. So the sleeping pills make the victim pliant yet a little coherent.'

Aileen shivered. 'Cold... So cold' As if struck by light-ning, Aileen straightened, 'We have two killers?'

'Perhaps—one to kill and one to help.'

A COUPLE OF HOURS LATER, A BLOKE SUITED UP IN A SHARP blazer and trousers arrived at the police station. It was Steve Johnson, Percy Winston's lawyer. He must have been an important client indeed for him to rush out to a town in the middle of nowhere.

He requested some privacy with his client.

CALLAN RETURNED TO HIS OFFICE AND TRIED TO MAKE heads or tails of the situation.

The dagger bugged him and as did the belt. Suppose it was Percy Winston who owned these two very distinctive items. Would he be stupid enough to use them to kill?

No, this killer had planned everything carefully. The belt might be an aberration but the killer would've had to have got the dagger along somehow.

Had Susan threatened the killer? Maybe she'd seen something and figured it out and the murderer had had less time to plan his second kill.

But why sound the alarm the night before? Cutting the lights the night of the murder could've helped the killer slip unnoticed from the murder scene, but the alarm…

Callan scratched his prickly beard. And slashing Aileen's tyres—was that significant in some way to the murder?

His gut told him these events weren't connected. There was something more happening here, undercurrents. Besides, Percy would have known the police could use fingerprints to find his identity. It wouldn't have taken them long to discover he'd owned the dagger.

Someone who'd planned everything so carefully wouldn't make that kind of slip. He wouldn't implicate himself by using a weapon that belonged to him and then leave that weapon behind for the police to see.

Callan stared out the window at the quiet town of Loch Fuar, lost in his thoughts.

Reaching for that infernal handset, he dialled the inspector with the Edinburgh police who'd been on the lookout for 'Dave Smith'. It didn't take long for the inspector to answer.

'Detective Inspector Cheryl Spiers'

'Inspector. I got yer email. I had a few questions for ye.'

'About the man you call Dave Smith?'

'Aye, I wanted to know if he had an accomplice.'

There was a brief pause before Inspector Spiers replied, 'Aye, he had a female partner. We aren't sure if they were romantically linked. You see, they each changed identities so very often, we couldn't keep tabs. They'd be married, brother-sister, colleagues...'

'The woman, his partner, what did she look like?'

'It's a futile attempt to decipher her physical appearance, Inspector Cameron. When I mean they changed identities they also changed appearances. His partner can alter her looks well, whether that's a wig, eye contacts, or changing the shape of her ears or adding a fake nose. We haven't been able to identify her features but we know her name.'

At the pause, Callan took a breath, stealing himself. 'What's her name?'

'Jocelyn Spencer, the surname I gather, is post marriage.'

'You wouldn't know her maiden name then?'

'No, she only got onto our radar after she'd married him.'

Callan drummed his hands, trying to take this information in. Was Martha, Jocelyn? Or was it Susan? That was an interesting thought.

'Where did you trace Dave Smith last?'

Inspector Spiers thought for a moment, 'London, around the area known as Canary Wharf.'

Someone in the background called for Spiers. The sound of shuffling and the bustle of a busy office came through the speaker. He'd been a part of that dance once.

Now, here he was in an office where you could hear angels whispering nothing but sermons of peace.

The line crackled before the inspector came online again. 'Sorry about that... So about Smith, he was last seen in London looking the same as he did then. He was alone, without his partner. But, what drew our attention to him was the number of people he was meeting.'

'What do ye mean?'

'Your pal was seen meeting a few renowned names as well as some ordinary people. They always had secretive meetings, our people couldn't get too close to know what they were discussing. He could sniff our people out.'

'Would you tell me any names?'

'Well, one of our officers recognised one of his acquaintances. It's a jeweller by the name of Jean Beaulieu.'

HALF AN HOUR LATER, CALLAN SAT IN AN INTERVIEW WITH Percy Winston and his lawyer, Johnson.

He turned to Johnson first. 'Fancy you being a Brit and able to get here so quickly. Our friend Richard here persists that he's from Canada, here on holiday.'

Johnson dismissed the question. 'Ask what's relevant, Mr Cameron.'

'Why did you lie about your name?'

No answer.

'Who did you threaten the evening before the second murder?'

'My client threatened no one.'

'Why were your fingerprints on the bedside lamp in an unfinished room at Dachaigh?'

'Can we see the evidence?'

Callan presented the report to the lawyer. All he did was request some more time with his client.

Stupid, sleazy lawyers, Callan cursed as he tapped his leg on the floor, with their pressed suits and their beady eyes and their gelled hair… They always got on his nerves. They'd fight for the Devil in court if he paid them enough.

Callan needed more evidence to tie the Grants to the crime scene. But the scene was clean, the murder well planned.

Had the killer killed before? That was unlikely, but killing at Loch Fuar? That was certainly an important piece of the puzzle. A small town with a negligible police force was a good place to kill.

That was the reason Siobhan had sought refuge here, away from prying eyes.

But the killer would know soon enough that Callan was no fool. He was good at his job, especially when it came to murder.

Keeping People Safe – Callan always stuck by those words.

CHARLES WYATT WOULD BE EASY TO FIND. THE LOCATION of his cottage was available for anyone to find. He enjoyed posting pictures of the fish he hauled in that area on social media.

Aileen sought out Isla. 'Fancy a quick road trip?'

'Twenty minutes!'

If Callan was preoccupied, the least Aileen could do was find information about the diamond belt. And Isla was the perfect partner – pushy enough to get blood out of a stone.

The tiny cottage stood by the loch, barely visible amidst the mountains that surrounded it. There were no other settlements that Aileen could see; it was a haven of privacy.

A maroon jeep coloured the damp landscape. It stood in front of the whitewashed stone cottage. The rest of the Highland scene was drenched in hues of blue and green.

Isla knocked on the door.

After what seemed like a full minute, they heard shuffling and then clicking as if someone were opening up multiple locks from the inside.

The door took some effort to pull open. It revealed an old man with a wrinkled face, white beard and hair.

He glanced at them with a quizzical look.

'Mr Wyatt?'

Charles Wyatt nodded.

Aileen flashed a friendly smile. He didn't seem a rich sort of person. In fact, there was a tear in his trousers, his boots had seen better days and the sweater he wore didn't seem to have been washed in a while.

Keeping her smile in place, she struck up a conversation. 'It's a beautiful view from here.'

'What's your business?' Charles wasn't one for small talk.

'Um, we…' Aileen hadn't quite decided how she'd sneak in her questions. She pointed a finger between Isla and herself.

'We love unique jewellery pieces. And um, the word is you've got a fascinating diamond-studded belt in your collection.'

Charles drew up to his full height just so he could look down his nose at the two ladies. 'And what would I do with this belt?'

Isla smiled. 'Oh, but I loved the diamond brooch you displayed as a part of your collections last year.' She sighed as if lost in happy old memories. 'The brooch that was worn by, who was it now…?'

'Augustus the Strong, King of Poland and the Elector of Saxony.' That answer fell from his lips like a well-rehearsed phrase.

He appraised the two again, finally came to a conclusion and nodded.

'It's best we take a walk.' With that, he strode ahead, skirting the edge of the loch waters.

Pebbles crunched under their feet, the ground wet from the rain that had added moisture to the Highland scenery.

'Beaulieu and Legrand were selling it to me. The jewellery traders?'

'Have you traded with them before?'

Charles shook his left hand to say no.

'They asked me to wait here and said they'd come to me with the belt. Safer that way – no one to nose about.' He regarded them again with scorn on his face.

But it was scorn directed towards Beaulieu and Legrand, Aileen realised.

'Humbugs, the pair of them! Never showed. They were to be here the day before last. Then I got a call to say they'd be here the day after. Hah! Still not here.'

'That's a shame,' Isla said.

'Shame!' His voice held some anger. 'They have my money! They bought the belt for me. And now? Where are they?'

Aileen assessed the situation quickly. 'Say, Mr Wyatt, I can tell you where they are. Would that help?'

A crooked smile cracked on the wrinkled old face, showing unclean yellow teeth.

'That'd be tremendously helpful, young lady. I have a thing or two to say to them.'

'In return, can you help me with something?'

THE TRIP HAD BEEN AN AMAZING SUCCESS FOR BOTH Charles Wyatt and Aileen. She almost danced into the police station to meet a harried-looking Callan.

'Where have ye been?'

Her smile widened. 'Being very busy and successful.'

Aileen placed a printout in front of Callan. 'That's your proof that this belt belonged to Beaulieu and Legrand.'

'How'd ye get that? Yer hacking skills won't give us sufficient evidence to bring the duo to justice.'

Aileen made a clicking sound, still too happy. 'Isla and I spoke with Charles Wyatt, who believes he's been duped. For a little bit of info about the pair's whereabouts, he gave us proof. Here are the emails between him and Beaulieu. And lookie here…' Aileen sang the last part out, 'Beaulieu himself says he's got the belt. He's included the catalogue number and product number in the email.'

Callan gave Aileen a doubtful look. 'Guess I'm getting Legrand and Beaulieu in.'

And with that he disappeared, the station door swinging behind him.

CALLAN CALLED ON ROBERT DAVIS TO GET LEGRAND AND Beaulieu in. Legrand made a huge fuss and howled out 'lawyer' quicker than the speed of light.

That was the last thing Callan wanted, another sleazy lawyer.

After placing the two in different rooms, Percy Winston's lawyer crossed over to Callan. 'We're ready to talk.'

He set up an interview for the third time.

'Promise to make a deal.'

Callan scoffed. 'First, talk.'

'Inspector, my client is a pillar of this society and an exemplary citizen—'

'Then he won't need a deal, will he?'

'I disagree,' the suited lawyer continued in his monotone voice.

'Bah!' Percy kicked the table. 'Shut up, you.'

Callan regarded him with a sceptical look. 'Are you willing to talk without a lawyer?'

The old man huffed. He was clearly at the end of his patience. After shooting his lawyer a dirty look, he turned a spiteful gaze on the inspector.

'I won't go into specifics. I won't! But I am Percy Winston from the south of England, not Canada. But I've never murdered any human being or animal in my life!'

Callan smirked. 'But ye know who did it.'

Percy's shoulders slumped. 'I thought I did. You see, my doctor's recommended I sleep early and rest well. So I do, sleep as deeply and early as I can. Samantha, my wife, does the same.'

'The murder?' Callan nudged him.

He regarded Callan. 'I blamed Jake that day. But Jacob's my son, and as a parent, I know he didn't do it.'

'Parents hold silly notions about their children. Most of them aren't naive, Mr Winston.'

'He didn't do it! I'm telling you. He couldn't have done the second murder!' Winston emphasised.

'Why?'

Percy shook his head. 'I cannot say.'

Callan changed his strategy.

'You own this dagger, don't you?'

Winston peered at the photograph of the murder

weapon. He shook his head, 'We don't. We used to, but we sold it. Check the records… I'm telling you - Jake couldn't have done it.'

Callan leaned back in his chair assessing the man in front of him. His seemingly harmless face looked well worn. But Callan's icy orbs scrutinised Percy.

The older man visibly wiggled in his seat, twiddling his fingers and looking around the banal room.

Suddenly leaning forward, Callan narrowed his eyes.

'No, no,' He said. 'Jake couldn't have done it. You'd know, given that you weren't asleep.'

Percy just shrugged. 'I don't understand what you're trying to imply. I repeat myself- I haven't killed either of them.'

Callan flashed his teeth like a lion about to pounce, 'You, Mr Winston, weren't tucked in bed as ye claim to be. You were too busy helping yer son commit a crime.'

CHAPTER FOURTEEN

Aileen sat on a chair in Callan's office. He regarded the innkeeper when he entered.

Her hair had been pinned back in place and her cheeks were slightly flushed. Apparently, Isla had returned to her bakery; the fiery redhead was nowhere to be seen. From what Callan had observed, the two women had grown a strong bond between them already. They almost always seemed to be in each other's company.

Callan told her what Percy had confessed.

'We do have the problem about motive,' Aileen pointed out.

Callan agreed. 'We don't know of any motive Jacob Winston could have had to kill Dave Smith or Susan Knight. And unless there's a connection, how did he know they'd be staying at the inn? The murders were pre-planned. At least, the first one was.'

'And how could he know Martha wouldn't walk into the room that night? He'd be caught red-handed.'

Callan snapped his fingers. 'Unless he drugged Martha also. She did spend all night asleep in the library.'

'Aye!' Aileen spoke quickly, with excitement. 'They were at the dining table together.'

'Interesting, yes – the killer could have slipped the first dose in then.' Callan tapped his chin then made a quick note on the incident board.

Turning to Aileen, he said, 'First I need to hear what Legrand and Beaulieu have to say about the belt.'

Aileen rose from her chair. It had probably dug holes into her back; it wasn't the most comfortable sitting place. 'Best of luck to you. I've got to get back.'

Callan nodded. 'See ye tomorrow then?'

'Aye.'

Aileen halted by the doorway. 'Gran called – she wanted to know what you did about your part of the deal.'

When Callan chuckled at Siobhan's persistence, Aileen breezed away with a small smile on her face. The road trip to see Charles Wyatt had evidently put her in a good mood.

CALLAN FOUND HIMSELF IN FRONT OF HIS INCIDENT BOARD, trying not to get overwhelmed by the red herrings littered all over this murder case. His intuition told him that the missing ring was closely associated with the murders but not in a straightforward way.

Pursing his lips, Callan read the board. He started with the first victim.

Dave Smith was a black-market dealer. His profession would have made him a few enemies. So was this murder a professional hit?

Callan had his doubts. The only other person was his 'female companion.'

Was Martha that woman? Or… Callan shuffled his feet, was it Susan?

Had someone targeted the pair and killed them?

Inspector Spiers from Edinburgh wasn't able to give him much information on Smith's partner.

Callan walked over to his files studying what data he'd gathered. This idea that Susan was Dave Smith's partner was indeed far-fetched — she had been associated with John Cook for over six years. And Dave, well, there was no record of his nuptials with Martha.

'Let's move to Susan,' Callan muttered to himself.

'Where did she earn all this money from? It's not all salary…' He trailed off.

What was she up to?

Callan cupped his chin, peering at the board. He thought back to the phone call he'd had with the Inspector in Edinburgh.

Dave Smith had been meeting various people in London, hadn't he? Percy Winston had a store in London. And Beaulieu and Legrand were also from London.

The inspector knew Beaulieu had met with Smith…

Callan snapped his fingers. 'Yes! Aileen's guests had to be well acquainted, at least a couple of them.'

He traced each photograph with his hands. Beaulieu had met Percy Winston at Barbara's Tea Shop.

That linked Dave Smith, Beaulieu and Percy Winston. And Beaulieu and Percy were the two people who owned the murder weapons.

'What's their motive?'

Perhaps a business deal went awry?

How much did the respective spouses know? And what about Susan?

Callan walked over to his laptop and read through the email Aileen had sent about Susan's accounts.

He read it again, trying to make sense of it.

'She says Susan was blackmailing someone. What are the chances this person is the killer?'

Callan sat back in his chair, the lingering residue of coffee leaving an acidic taste in his mouth.

He closed his eyes, trying to think of the tall elegant woman he'd known as Susan Knight. Aileen had called her personable. But based on the current events, Callan could file her personality on good acting.

His next question was: why Loch Fuar?

He stood, pacing in his cramped office space. Loch Fuar was a great place to bury a body. They couldn't possibly search the entire landscape.

'Someone's chosen this location purposely. But it's more than the quaintness of this town...'

Callan paused. 'It has to be the diamond ring!'

Storming over to the board, he looked at Beaulieu. This man was a geologist, married to a jeweller. And Percy Winston was an antique dealer. Add this to Dave Smith's black-market expertise, how long would it take for them to hear about these diamonds?

Surely thieves were a step ahead of police inspectors, as much as Callan hated to admit it. And the Inspector who'd been on the case to locate these diamonds was an eejit.

They planned to steal them...

And their family members?

What was their involvement in this?

'I'm telling you — Jake couldn't have done it.' Percy Winston had been so sure when he'd said that during the interview.

And he wasn't lying. Callan closed his eyes, trying to picture the interiors of the inn.

Percy and Samantha Winston were positioned nearest to the Control Room. Opposite them was Susan and John's room. Had they been awake — which based on their statements, they weren't — they could've seen Susan and John leaving the room.

So why was Percy lying? Unless it had been Jake who'd led Susan out. Or Legrand?

Beaulieu was too short to tie the belt around Susan's neck, even in her inebriated condition.

Callan tapped the board, remembering what Aileen had told him about that night. She'd seen Jake's torchlight move towards the stairs as he headed from his father's room door...

Or was he at his father's room door?

Yeah, gosh, yeah, Callan grinned. He'd finally found the link.

ISLA ASKED AILEEN TO WAIT TILL SHE CLOSED UP HER bakery for the day.

'Did you make any headway?' Isla wanted to know.

Aileen made a face that told her she wasn't sure. 'Callan's interviewing Beaulieu and Legrand about the belt now. But there are so many other questions that need answering...'

Isla paused her aggressive attack with a duster on the glass showcase. 'Like what?'

'Oh! Where do I begin? The biggest question I ask myself is what's the motive? Every murder needs one. Unless the killer's just doing it for fun.' That thought made goosebumps pop on Aileen's skin.

Isla shook her head. 'That's unlikely. There too many details that the killer needed to plan and there's a reason why they've done it here in Loch Fuar.'

'Aye. Besides, don't the ones that kill for fun crave a good chase? That's what I've heard. I'm no student of psychology, but serial killers and such would find a much more exciting chase in a city. A place where crime is rampant.'

Aye, you're assured of a diligent inspector who'll work to track you down. Not to mention, more people to kill.'

They lapsed into silence as they each thought things through.

Aileen jerked up. 'Oh, I didn't think about this before!'

'Think about what?'

Aileen waved an exasperated hand at her. 'Martha Smith! She told me – she told me she was no good in the kitchen.'

'So?' Isla checked her phone. 'Oh shit! Daniel's asked if I can get home quick. The wee one's bawling her eyes out.'

After a brief roll of her eyes, Isla added, 'He can't handle tears. You should've seen it when I was pregnant. I teared up so many times. He'd run out of the house screaming!'

Aileen laughed at the image of a tall muscular man running out on the street because his wife was crying.

What had she been about to say? Aileen snorted. Forget it. Her friend needed her.

Isla cracked up. 'Oh, Daniel!' She placed a hand on her heart. 'I'll drop you off quick if you don't mind.'

'Of course, it's fine. You should get back to Carly before Daniel runs out of the house!'

Laughing together, they were soon on their way to Dachaigh, though they sobered up and manoeuvred back to serious talk soon enough.

'I can't understand why Percy Winston says his son couldn't have done the second murder,' Isla remarked after Aileen gave her a quick rundown of everything Callan had told her.

'Or why Beaulieu or Legrand would kill Dave Smith or Susan Knight.'

Isla thought it out. 'Actually, did you notice how Charles Wyatt said he was expecting them to turn up the day before last?'

When Aileen nodded, she continued, 'I wonder why they didn't. They've been asked not to leave town, but they wouldn't have technically left Loch Fuar to get to his cottage. It's just a few miles from here.'

Aileen caught up. 'You think they couldn't meet up with him because the belt had been stolen.'

'Or they wanted to use it to murder Susan.'

'Isla, why would they do that? It's self-sabotage. They ended up losing the belt as evidence to the police, and Charles Wyatt is a serious collector of jewellery pieces. If he badmouths them, no matter their reputation, their business is sunk into the ground.'

Just like mine. Aileen didn't voice the last part.

'Well, you're right. It's all above my head.'

Aileen chuckled. 'You're a smart woman. And great at milking people for gossip.'

Isla snickered. 'Oh, it's all in the practice.'

'Where'd you find out about the brooch?'

Isla waved a dismissive hand. 'A little bit of research. You're not the only one who can dig up dirt.'

Laughing with her new best friend felt good.

When they reached Dachaigh, Aileen bid her friend goodnight and skipped over to the old fence, humming to herself as she pushed the gate open.

She looked up, breathing in the refreshing fragrance of primroses. Her grandmother's inn... She caressed it fondly with her gaze. Her inn now.

An inn which currently housed a murderer, Aileen's mind reminded her.

Dismissing that horrid thought, she proceeded up the tiled pathway amidst beautiful blooming flowers.

The golden glow of her inn engulfed her in a warm hug. But contrary to the noisy bustling establishment she'd hoped to be running, all was quiet.

She hoped Callan caught the killer soon. She wished for a better and refreshing batch of guests. Next time, she'd do a background check and she'd install more security cameras.

Aileen rolled her eyes as she set her purse on the kitchen counter. More security cameras would be a pain. Just like her car tyres, they would take a while to arrive and she would need a technician to fix them up.

Daniel could handle the wiring but they'd need an IT technician to connect the cameras up to her servers.

And the keys, Aileen smiled to herself. Like Callan had told her, she needed to be careful about those as well.

Thinking about keys, Aileen was reminded of the blackout. Why had it been necessary?

Jake Winston had been roaming about that night, and he had no alibi – his wife had been with John Cook and Martha Smith.

There were just too many links that didn't add up.

The other anomaly that bugged her was about the drug. Susan Knight was an intelligent woman. Visiting an unfinished room was odd enough, but accepting a drink from someone she didn't know? In an inn where someone had been killed?

And from what they knew, Susan hadn't suffered from insomnia or any problems of that sort.

Aileen hated confusion. When in doubt, she thought it was best to list down all your outstanding questions and details. She'd followed this practice through all her tough cases, and this time would be no different.

CALLAN HAD LONG UNDERSTOOD THAT SHIFTS AT THE police station were non-existent. Especially when the police only had a three-man army.

Rory had had to leave because he had his grandweans to babysit, and Robert Davis had a newborn Callan didn't think he should be away from.

And anyway, hadn't he craved a real case when he'd had to stay late at the station just to resolve the issue of where Douglas's cat had disappeared to?

Callan spread his legs as he slumped on his swivelling chair. It had been quite the day.

It had been a while since he'd been in a formal interview, grilling murder suspects. And now he'd interviewed three suspects in one day.

Percy Winston had been easy enough to break, but Louis Legrand and Jean Beaulieu... He didn't know what to do about those two. They'd asked for a lawyer immediately, and those lawyers were now discussing matters with them, in separate interviewing rooms.

Callan needed a strategy to work them. Perhaps he could ask Rory to return, or even Robert might be helpful, though neither of them had had much experience with murder either.

The emails Charles Wyatt had provided were enough to prove that the diamond belt had been in the possession of Legrand and Beaulieu. The two Frenchmen had to talk to Callan about that.

When Callan entered Room A, he found Legrand sitting absolutely erect beside his even stiffer lawyer. The Frenchman gave him a look of disinterest, but Callan knew it was a disguise for fear. He feared being caught.

The lawyer assessed Callan down his long pointy nose. He looked like he'd rather be anywhere else.

His thin-lipped mouth opened. 'Mr Legrand would like to cooperate with you if—'

The lawyer broke off when Callan waved his hands.

'I need to know yer client has the information I need before I make a deal.' Callan sat back in the squeaky chair and folded his left leg over the right. 'I've proof that the weapon used to murder Susan Knight belonged to your client. How long will it take for me to pin this on him… Or perhaps on his spouse?'

His last words got a reaction out of Legrand; he jerked up in his chair and finally met Callan's graze. 'Jean didn't do anything!' His voice was like the crack of a whip.

A small smile played on Callan's lips. 'Oh?' He looked at Legrand. 'How would ye know that?'

The lawyer propped his hand in between the two over the table. As if timing out the first bout in a boxing match.

Like he was explaining to a small child, the lawyer met Callan's gaze and said, 'Inspector, I assure you what my client has to say will be of assistance to you.'

Callan's chuckle sounded like the Devil's, echoing around the room. 'So he knows who's the killer?'

Legrand and his lawyer looked at each other. The lawyer piped in, 'No, but we know who isn't.'

Callan leaned forward with both elbows on the desk. 'Telling me your client had nothing to do with murder isn't enough.'

'Inspector, we have logical reasoning for that claim.'

'Aye?' Callan mocked.

'As long as you keep this off the record, my client will cooperate.'

'Him not cooperating will land him in a deeper puddle than he's in now.'

Legrand fidgeted in his chair, turned to his lawyer and said, 'Don't play with my life!'

Righting himself in his chair, the lawyer continued, 'Inspector, my clients are well known in their fields as jewellers. Such a scandal would—'

'Talk first – we'll consider a deal later. Unless your client's killed people. Then there's no mercy for him.'

'I haven't!' came a stubborn mumble.

'You willing to talk now, Legrand?' Callan mocked him.

'Inspector, please. Let me explain this to you.'

The lawyer's snotty accent was getting on Callan's nerves.

He made a tsk sound and told him, 'It better be good.'

AILEEN COULDN'T WAIT TO GET DINNER OUT OF THE WAY SO she could get back to investigating.

Jake and Anne sat at the table, holding hands but not speaking, each lost in their thoughts. Samantha had retired to bed, saying her head ached.

Martha Smith walked in – more like sauntered in – and approached the kitchen counter where Aileen stood. 'Do you make your own bread?'

Aileen laughed. 'I'm no good at baking. My friend Isla is a genius.'

'Oh!' Martha laughed as well. 'Does she own the bakery in town?'

'Aye, have you been there?'

'I walked past it. I love walking around town.' Martha waved her hand, dismissing the topic, then steered away as if avoiding Aileen all together. Something wasn't right.

Why did she look so sure of herself today? Where was

the grieving widow? And surely a person fond of baking bread would have ventured into the bakery rather than just passing by?

Aileen drummed her fingers on the counter. What was it that Martha had said once before about the kitchen?

I wouldn't know where to begin.

So what was she doing with Anne Grant the night Susan was killed? Could they be discussing bread or something more sinister? Perhaps, Aileen bit her lips, it was a ruse to ensure they had alibis. Could Anne have dragged Martha along just so she'd be accounted for at the time of the murder?

The Winstons were indeed playing a sinister game.

The oil she'd lined the pot with shimmered. The crackle distracted Aileen from her unceasing thoughts.

She hoped spaghetti and meatballs would lift her guests' spirits. At least those guests who weren't at the police station.

Once she was done, she would get to that list of questions she'd vowed to make earlier. That would help her sort this nasty business out.

IN TOWN, THE SUN BEGAN TO BID FAREWELL FOR THE DAY, but Callan was still making hay. He was even enjoying it.

Legrand's lawyer was just like his client. That made Callan remember all those funny online posts about dogs and their owners looking alike. The lawyer was expensive, which just told Callan that his client was no stranger to legal issues.

The lawyer cleared his throat at the small smile on Callan's face.

Callan spoke. 'Let's hear the tale then. Keep it short so I don't doze off.'

'Inspector!' The lawyer sat straighter as his attitude turned indignant. 'I assure you it's not a *tale.*'

He continued after a pause as if preparing for his impending speech.

'My client came to Loch Fuar for business. As I told you before, he is a revered jeweller. Legrand and Beaulieu have high-paying clients who admire them for their discretion and their efficiency.'

The lawyer pointed to the emails Charles had provided. 'Charles Wyatt is a new customer and thus my client agreed to come up to the Highlands to hand over his piece.'

'When did this happen?'

'They spoke on the phone and decided to meet at the cottage on the edges of the loch. Wyatt owns the place, and it is discreet enough to conduct such delicate business.'

Callan nodded.

'My client and his spouse – who is also his business partner – took a flight from London to Glasgow, then boarded the train to Loch Fuar. They flew premium class and used the first-class compartment in the train. They were the only ones there, no other passengers.'

'And from the station?'

'My client hired a car. They needed one to get to the cottage.'

'And why was the transfer of the belt delicate business?'

'Inspector,' the lawyer admonished, 'it's a diamond-studded belt made from the most exquisite stones. It's worth a lot.'

'So why risk bringing it here?'

'For discretion'

'Who knew about this exchange?'

The lawyer cast a look at Legrand, who stared impassively at the desk.

'Just Mr Legrand and Mr Beaulieu.'

Callan narrowed his eyes, 'Are you sure? None of their employees had a clue?'

'No, this visit was classified as a holiday in their calendar.'

'But a holiday this isn't.'

Callan placed a picture of the diamond belt on the table.

'Tell me what happened to the belt'

'My client Mr Legrand and Mr Beaulieu had come over to the Highlands to conduct business. They were to go over to the cottage to meet Charles Wyatt. The night before they'd agreed to meet, Mr Beaulieu opened the case to make sure everything was in place.'

'And was it?'

'I'm afraid not. The belt was gone and someone had broken the case.'

Callan scratched all this down in his notebook. 'Why didn't they report this to the police?'

The lawyer sat up straighter, 'As I said, Wyatt wanted to practice discretion. Going to the police would have alerted the world about the theft and essentially tarnished my clients' reputation.'

'Instead, they kept mum?'

The lawyer shook his head. 'So they asked Charles Wyatt for more time.'

Callan let out a breath. 'And how had they kept the diamond-studded belt guarded the entire time?'

'My clients never left the belt alone, and they hadn't let anyone clean their room. But the night of the alarm, they'd found their bedroom window open.'

WHEN CALLAN FINALLY CLOSED THE DOOR BEHIND HIM, HIS entire body craved a hit of coffee. So he brewed one and stood in front of the incident board.

The interview with Legrand had been a long one. And he still had to talk with Beaulieu. But the more information Callan gathered, the more he was sure that the Frenchmen seemed incapable of murder.

For one, they were too snotty. And for another, murder was messy. Legrand was so concerned about his reputation, there was no way he'd risk that sort of scandal. He was the sort who'd pay a professional to do it for him if he did ever need to get rid of someone. And he would be nowhere near the murder scene; he just wasn't that sort of a person.

Beaulieu, Callan mused, was an oddball. He did show some compassion but adopted Legrand's attitude whenever it pleased him.

Callan made sure he drank the last drop of his coffee before he headed to the next interview. He was knackered!

DINNER HAD BEEN ANOTHER QUIET AFFAIR.

John Cook had played with his food but had managed to eat some after Martha Smith urged him on. Perhaps, Aileen mused, their shared experience of losing a spouse had formed a connection between them.

Jake and Anne had retired upstairs, still not having spoken a single word apart from the 'thank you' and 'good-night'. They continued to speak in Canadian accents, never once breaking the act.

Aileen looked out the kitchen window. The green

moors were turning dark as the sun set under the horizon, the waters of the loch falling silent after glittering under the sun all day.

What had Jake been up to the night the lights went off? And why did Percy think he couldn't have committed the murder?

And why Susan, a female rights activist? All the news articles Aileen had found spoke highly about her. She had made a huge impact, especially in the lives of women who'd found themselves with no money or shelter over their heads, though she supposed Susan would also have made enemies among those women's abusive ex-partners.

But all in all, she was a likeable person. So why murder her? What was the motive?

And seeing all the nastiness in the world, she'd have been a careful woman. Would such a woman have accepted a drink from another guest when they were all under investigation for murder? Had someone threatened her?

They were all just questions. But somewhere in her head, her mind screamed. It told her the answer was right there, waiting to be found.

But she couldn't see it. She could only ask more questions. Who had drugged Dave Smith? Had they also drugged Martha so she wouldn't walk in on the murderer? Could Jake have slipped something in their drinks at dinner?

CALLAN SCRATCHED HIS CHIN. HE'D UNDERESTIMATED Beaulieu but now he'd asked the right questions, he was finally getting some answers. The thing was, his answers matched exactly with Legrand's. They didn't seem rehearsed – just the truth.

Except Beaulieu had told him he'd left the window slightly ajar the night the alarm had sounded. The room had turned too stuffy for him.

'And what's your client's relationship with Mr Percy Winston?'

'My client doesn't know any Percy Winston.' Compared to Legrand's snooty lawyer, this one spoke like a robot in a monotone voice. It was only the rise and fall of his chest that told Callan he was indeed human.

'Does your client know Richard Grant then?'

'Not personally he doesn't. Mr Grant is staying at the inn, a few rooms down from my client.'

'But they were seen together in the tea room in town, nice and cosy.'

Callan flashed his teeth when the lawyer called it a bluff.

'Ye should know, people in a small town such as this one thrive on gossip, and they don't like the ugly stamp of murder on their home either. And Barbara's a good friend of mine. So she told me.' As had Aileen, but he didn't want to bring her name into it.

The lawyer waved a hand. 'It was a brief run-in.'

Callan laughed. 'Having a good blether the entire afternoon? That's hardly brief. I've got multiple witnesses that say you had yer heads stuck together for hours as ye poured over some papers.'

At that revelation, the lawyer asked for another consultation with his client.

But Callan's smile only grew bigger as he exited the room. He knew he'd got Beaulieu good and proper; the man had undeniably committed a crime, but was it murder? Callan wasn't sure.

AT LONG LAST AILEEN TRUDGED UP THE STAIRS, GLAD TO BE finally retiring to her chambers. She promised herself a nice warm soak in her bathtub when this case was behind her. It wouldn't be much longer, she hoped.

She could feel the stress building on her shoulders. These were trying times, but they'd taught her a lot. Like security and its importance. Aileen sneered at herself.

Opening the door to her small study, she slumped on the chair in front of her laptop. Her laptop was so much better than the computer at the police station. But even if the police-issued computer was old and clunky, at least it gave her quick and ethical access to police files.

Aileen pulled out her classic yellow notepad; it was what she always used to sort things out. Though funnily enough, she hadn't used it when she'd decided to move to Loch Fuar. This move had been a quick, impromptu one, but despite the current circumstances, the decision had still been a good one.

She thought about the positives: she owned an inn, had made a best friend, could breathe in fresh Highland air every day and admire the shimmering stars in the night sky, so much more vivid here than in the city.

Letting out a breath, she brought herself to the present.

She listed down the names of her guests and thought about each of them.

The stiff-backed Legrand, and his shorter more compassionate spouse Beaulieu.

Richard Grant, aka Percy Winston, and his entire family, who'd lied about their identity. Why had they done that?

That brought her to Dave Smith, the first murdered

guest. Thinking back to the scene she'd discovered sent a shiver down her spine.

His wife was a weird sort. She'd cried alright, but there was something she seemed to be hiding. It was in her stance and the way she spoke. If she hadn't been drugged, why would a wife spend the night sleeping in an uncomfortable chair when she'd come on holiday with her husband? Hadn't they wanted to enjoy the weekend together? His birthday weekend at that.

Aileen thought back to that night and the strange disappearance of her keys.

Just to make sure, she jingled the keys in her right trouser pocket. They hadn't disappeared again. Whoever had snatched them – taken them twice no less – had completed their work.

Who had stolen her grandmother's ring? And who could have known it was worth stealing in the first place?

Lastly, Aileen noted down the name John Cook. What was he up to in this entire rigmarole? He was a lawyer, someone who worked for women's rights. It was how he'd met his wife.

But he wasn't the most personable man. He hadn't mingled with the other guests, though not everyone wanted to talk to strangers. She knew enough about the need some people had to be left alone – sometimes she was one of them.

Her last guest, and the second murder victim, Susan Knight, was another mystery, though she'd seemed friendlier than John.

The woman she'd spoken to at the shelter had mentioned a fight, though they'd seemed civilised with each other. Maybe it was just work pressure that had wedged a problem in their relationship. They'd come to

Loch Fuar to get away from work, hadn't they? John had mentioned so to Callan.

That brought her to why Susan had gone to the unoccupied room. Who had she met up there?

And all of these questions led to a single one: what was the motive behind it all?

Aileen drummed her fingers as she picked out her interwoven thoughts. Any one of her guests could be the killer. They just had to have been able to get the drug into the victims…

She tapped a steady rhythm, her left leg dancing along. The killer had to have had patience, to wait for the right moment to strike.

Aileen remembered the footsteps she was sure she'd heard at around midnight, the night Dave Smith was murdered. Who could that be?

Maybe the killer had an ally…

The speed of her rhythm picked up; her leg began to sway aggressively…

An ally – perhaps a parent; a spouse? No, that was too obvious and dangerous.

Could one of her guests be a hired hit? But then there would have had to be a connection between Dave and Susan.

She thought about Susan and the opportunities someone might have had to dose her with a sleeping drug.

Suddenly her tapping came to an end. Her legs halted their nervous beat and stilled.

Aileen pulled open Susan's financial records Callan had sent her.

Oh yes, yes!

Susan wasn't just a smarty, Aileen peered at those regular payments from the same account, she was a very good blackmailer…

Aileen stared at her notes again. It couldn't be, could it?

Callan still couldn't figure it out, nor did he entirely agree with his theories about the murders.

He wasn't an expert on family secrets, but could Beaulieu have plans to sell the diamond ring and keep them from his husband? The chances of him keeping anything from that prick Legrand were minimal.

And Percy? He'd shared everything with Jake. He'd have to.

That left Samantha, Anne, Martha and John.

Did any of them have a motive?

Samantha had one speeding ticket in her name. How could such a woman kill someone?

And Samantha's daughter-in-law was no different. Anne Winston was a scaredy-cat, too frail to handle an incapacitated Susan.

Legrand, as Callan had put it before, was too snooty to kill someone especially in a way that drew blood. He wouldn't want blood on his pristine clothes.

Martha, her life was in obscurity. Jocelyn, that's what Spiers had called Dave's partner. But Dave's murder showed no vengeance. And why would she kill Susan? Unless Dave and Susan were… Involved.

Again Susan's murder had no vengeance. Generally, a betrayed wife would question the woman with whom her husband had…

Unless, unless… Jocelyn… Where had he read that name before?

These murders were a result of jealousy surely, but not

the kind that dealt with love. No, the motive was stronger… It was money.

That left John Cook. He had played the part of a grieving widower but hadn't shown a flicker of remorse for Martha's loss.

Susan had kept secrets from him, perhaps leading to their disagreements… Or had she?

Callan scrambled over to Susan's financials.

One name on his mind — Cook.

In his desperation, Callan flipped the pages, but couldn't seem to find the name.

At wit's end, he sat back, forcing himself to breathe. There was no use getting agitated. The answer was at his fingertips, he just had to find the evidence.

Evidence that would implicate John Cook and Martha Smith.

Or, Callan sneered as the name finally popped onto the page: John Cook and his cousin Jocelyn Cook.

Jocelyn Cook who'd been paying Susan Knight black-mail money…

CHAPTER FIFTEEN

Callan sat staring at a sweating Beaulieu. The man grimaced, looking out of place in that plain interview room.

Jean Beaulieu had spoken – in fact, he'd sung like a bird during spring. And lo and behold, Callan had discovered some precious information, though it wasn't about the murders. Now he wanted to know:

'Tell me, Mr Beaulieu, where is the ring?'

Beaulieu looked at his lawyer — The man said, 'What ring, Inspector?'

'The one your client planned to steal.'

Beaulieu blinked, gripping the edge of the table, muttering something in french.

'Ah Mr Beaulieu, I cannae understand ye. Do you have the ring?'

Beaulieu shook his head, 'Non! I don't know where your ring is.'

Callan was done with interviews. His eyes hurt from all the strain. And his bloody right knee protested from the pacing.

But he was as excited as Aileen was.

Callan stood up and started pacing again, despite his protesting knee.

Aye, now it made better sense.

Beaulieu didn't know where the ring was and despite his refusal, he'd met Richard that day to discuss something. Callan could bet his meagre annual salary, it was about the ring.

Callan rubbed his hands over his worn face.

One of the guests had to know about the existence of this ring. So why kill two guests to steal it?

That part bothered him.

Aye, that itch in his gut was right. The ring and the murders: they weren't as interwoven as he'd thought them to be.

Callan stood again and glanced at his incident board. Eight suspects stared back at him. Aileen wasn't one of them, he was sure. And with what Beaulieu had told him, he was down to a select few.

He was down to one.

Yes – yes it fitted together!

The troubled knee was long forgotten as Callan flew out of his office and off to hunt down the killer.

Aileen sat staring at her yellow notepad. It made sense to her now!

The killer had a strong alibi but also enough motivation to do it. How could Aileen not have seen it before!

The lies, the ruse and most importantly the slight flinch in her body language.

Oh, how it came together in her head. It explained the footsteps also, but Aileen frowned. It didn't explain the theft of her gran's ring.

Maybe Callan could help her piece that part together. In her excitement, Aileen fumbled for her phone, but it wasn't in her pocket. Where had she put it?

Just then she heard it – the creak of the floorboards. It sounded close. Too close. The hair on the back of her neck rose, alert.

As if on cue, the door to her bedroom across the hall opened. It was a distinctive sound.

Aileen hunched behind the door of her study room and looked around for anything to help her protect herself.

With a wooden ruler, she stepped out of her tiny study.

It had been a bad idea to step out. The ruler made her look like a teacher whose bark was way worse than her bite.

There was a murderer in their midst. A sane human being would have locked themselves in the study and called the police. But in her excitement, Aileen had not only stepped out but moved towards the footsteps, to her bedroom.

Aileen didn't turn the lights on. To her utter dismay, it was a moonless night and the blinds were pulled shut. Her eyes struggled to adjust from the stark glow of the lamp in her study room.

Damn her phone! Where was it when she needed it? If only she could reach Callan.

A bulb flickered inside her head. The bedside table! That's where she'd left it to recharge.

As if hearing her thought, the phone flashed, like a beacon of light at the end of the tunnel. A message. But what the light also revealed was the lone figure standing in the dark abyss at the other end of her bedroom.

Before Aileen could steel herself, the man lunged at her and she crashed hard on the floor, his bulk squeezing the air out of her lungs.

Shooting pain zipped through her back, and a huge rough hand landed on her mouth. 'Quiet,' a gruff voice threatened. 'One wrong move and I'll snap your little neck like a twig.'

Hot breath washed over Aileen's face. It felt like the breath of a demon from hell. Somewhere in the dark, death loomed over her.

'You thought you were so clever? Assisting that twat and staring me down during that shit you call dinner.'

Was this it? Would he end her? He had to. She knew who he was; she'd recognise that voice anywhere, and he hadn't dared mask his disinterested tone. Only now his voice sounded colder than the frozen water of Loch Fuar in the peak of winter.

A shudder ran down her spine; Aileen felt her hands going cold.

Fear – this is what real fear felt like. This was the end.

Aileen struggled but she had no chance. Her fidgeting landed her nowhere close to freeing her legs, and he'd pinned both her wrists with one hand.

'Shut up, you bitch!'

Was it wise to talk to him? Try to coax him into letting her go?

He pressed her head further into the ground and her back screamed with terrifying sparks of pain. Her hands started to fall dead from the lack of blood supply.

A crash sounded from down below, and a heavy stomping of feet told her someone was approaching.

But was it a foe or a friend?

Her captor released the grip on her mouth only to wrap his iron-like paws around her throat.

'What did you do?' He banged her head on the floor as if she were a rag doll.

Aileen fought for dear breath. She almost gagged; her head sang with pain.

In his fury, the man's grip on her wrists lessened. Struggling but still tenacious, Aileen found her opportunity to strike. With all her might, she jabbed her elbow into his head. It was a blind strike but his grip on her throat loosened.

Gulping in as much oxygen as she could, Aileen shoved her hands into his chest.

Someone banged on the door but it didn't budge.

Encouraged by her success, Aileen used her elbow again, trying to set at least one of her legs free. But her attacker was ready – he caught her and twisted her arm at a bad angle. Aileen swore she heard something snap and howled with pain.

Another crash sounded in the distance, and the pounding on her door began again.

Blood roared in Aileen's ears, deafening her to any other sounds apart from her war cry.

She tumbled over, rolling across the floor. Her throat burned and her vision didn't seem right even in the dark. Her elbows hurt where they'd been scraped raw, and so did her knees. Everything hurt.

But adrenaline throbbed through Aileen's body, flooding her muscles with energy. She jumped up on her feet to attack the man.

But she lost her footing as the door to her left flew off its hinges and another burly figure barged in.

The shadow lunged towards her attacker. She could

barely make out what was happening, but the sounds told her they fought vigorously.

Stumbling over her numb feet, with a flicker of determination egging her on, Aileen found her way to the light switch.

Fumbling and cursing, she turned it on.

Everything went still for a moment as bright light blinded the room.

After a brief pause, the two men on the floor continued to wrestle.

Never before had she had a man fight for her – now two men were brawling in her bedroom. That amusing thought went out the door when John Cook shoved Callan away.

The inspector countered with a punch to John's face but he deflected with a blow of his own. They went at each other again, panting heavily.

A few splatters of blood flew across the room. A second later, blood oozed out of John's nose. Callan was in no better shape, his own river of blood staining the front of his black shirt.

What could be done when an officer of the law was in a wrestling match with a murderer?

When John punched Callan so hard that he landed on his back, Aileen's revved body acted on its own accord.

She didn't know how she did it, especially with no practice.

Forgetting her aches and pains, Aileen jumped forward and raised her leg to strike. Her kick landed where it had meant to – below John Cook's belt. It might have been the oldest trick in the book but it worked.

Apparently, her limbs weren't done. Perhaps the frustration of the previous days had caught up to her, but like a ninja, Aileen thrust a second hard kick at the same spot.

That had her former captor crumbling to the ground with a loud howl.

While the old Aileen would have doubted her actions, this Aileen smirked with vengeance on her face.

She glimpsed at Callan, who was still sprawled on the floor, his trouser legs hitched up to his calves. A shocked gasp escaped her before he covered his legs back up. He'd walked differently alright but she'd never have guessed he was an amputee!

Of course, there was a story there, but some stories were personal, and no matter how curious she was, she'd developed a new respect for Callan throughout all this – he was more than he let on beneath that black broody facade. He could tell her about it when he was ready, whenever that might be.

For now, she'd just enjoy feeling superhuman while it lasted.

CALLAN JUMPED UP, GOT HIS HANDCUFFS OUT AND LOOKED at John with some pity, making a note never to get on Aileen's nerves. The women in the Mackinnon family weren't to be messed with. Especially the woman who stood panting beside him.

He'd watched in awe, his jaw hanging open, as she'd slammed her foot into John Cook's weakest part not once but twice. The poor sod was still wriggling on the floor screaming bloody murder, his tears evidence of the burning pain he felt. Maybe, Callan thought, that was exactly what he deserved after killing one man and then his lady.

He'd definitely add this unusual end to his report.

He looked at Aileen with a shrewd smile. 'I'll call

Robert up, ask him to get another set of handcuffs along. We'll need them for Martha Smith.'

Aileen grinned back at him, apparently only too eager to put this horrid business behind her.

As if on their own accord, Callan's right hand slipped into Aileen's. He squeezed it… In reassurance? Callan certainly hoped so.

He felt blood seep out of the cut on his lips. Callan knew he'd have to explain things to the innkeeper soon. But for now, he huffed out a satisfactory breath, ready to lead the unwelcome killer away from *home*.

WHAT A NIGHT! LOCH FUAR'S ENTIRE POLICE FORCE HAD descended on her doorstep, though Aileen's mind had shut off somewhere between Rory Macdonald arriving and Callan leading the two criminals out of Dachaigh. She ached all over, barely able to stand upright.

Rory Macdonald had assembled everyone in the drawing room. He paced, maintaining a vigil, not for invaders but for the group he guarded.

Samantha and Anne stood looking silently out into the night, while Jake had tried his best to argue with Rory, demanding Percy's return. Aileen would never have thought the white-haired, grandfatherly superior police officer could be so cold and assertive. He'd shut Jake down immediately.

RORY NOW REGARDED THE YOUNG AILEEN MACKINNON. She'd proved herself a resourceful individual. Siobhan had been right about her grandchild; Aileen had indeed risen to the challenge and emerged victorious, despite the nefarious plans of her guests.

The Winstons, he observed, stood tall with pride, as if no one could touch them. As if the dark cloud had passed.

His grandweans might have thought he was a pushover, but Rory knew how to keep an eye on things. He'd reviewed those interviews Callan had conducted, and he had noticed the same pride in all of the men questioned: Jean Beaulieu, Louis Legrand and Percy Winston.

They'd each smirked, looked superior and hidden behind their stiff-collared lawyers. What they didn't know was they'd been digging their own graves, and now that Callan had just come striding back into the drawing room, the cat would soon be out of the bag.

CALLAN GAVE RORY A QUICK NOD BEFORE HIS GAZE FELL ON Aileen. She looked beat. Her trousers were ripped and so were the sleeves of her shirt, while her hair looked like a rooster had nested in it. He was sure she'd have her fair share of bruises tomorrow.

The rest of this lot, well... He was going to relish this...

'Hand the ring over, and you'll see the light of day quicker.'

Jake jerked upright as if he'd been slapped.

'Excuse me?' he spat.

Callan relaxed his posture, a smirk playing on his lips. 'You can drop the accent, too. Your father did.'

Jake took a defensive pose as if readying for a fight. 'This is how I talk—'

'I've got a report to write, people to book with murder and I want the ring that belongs to Ms Mackinnon's grandmother. I know you have it; you know you have it. Save me time and hand it over.'

'He's no thief!' Samantha Winston jumped to her son's rescue. She'd dropped her fake accent.

Callan let it go and instead turned to Anne. 'I can have you checked or you could show me the golden chain you have tucked under your shirt, Mrs Winston.'

Anne didn't move.

'I'm calling our lawyer,' Samantha began.

'Go ahead and do that. I've got evidence and witnesses willing to speak.'

Anne raised a trembling hand to the thin golden chain around her neck and gripped it tight.

'There's no evidence,' she mumbled.

'It won't do ye any good to protect them,' Callan told her, nodding to the rest of her family. 'All they'll do is pin this on ye and walk away.'

Jake finally spoke, flustered, 'She wears that chain every day. You cannot blame an innocent woman.'

'Then please show us what that chain holds.'

It was an open challenge. With two members of the police force in attendance, Jake could do nothing. He'd declared Anne innocent for all to hear.

Anne's gaze flittered from Samantha to Jake. She looked unsure, shaking like a timid bird.

'Come on, lassie,' Rory urged her in a grandfatherly way. 'Nothing to worry about if ye're innocent.'

With trembling hands, she lifted the chain, and as it emerged from under her collar, the glint of diamonds caught the light.

Callan heard Aileen gasp.

Despite her tired eyes and sore body, Aileen looked at the diamond like a star-struck woman. She couldn't believe she'd never seen the jewellery piece before.

The engagement ring would be called 'modest' by some, but it did look exquisite. Her grandfather had truly designed it with love, perfect for his short yet witty bride.

A solitaire threw dancing rainbow lights onto the wall, clear and bright like the sun. Smaller minute crystals sparkled around the lone stone as if dancing in rhythm to the sun's beam.

Aileen's heart sighed; Siobhan had been the centre of her grandfather's universe.

Callan snorted. 'Well, that's an unexpected discovery.'

Aileen snapped out of her romantic haze and focused once more on the events transpiring in the room.

Jake's hand shook, and he looked dumbfounded – because he knew about the ring or because he didn't?

Anne's trembling hands still gripped the chain and her gaze fixed on her husband's.

'Duped – we've been duped,' he sputtered out lies. 'Beaulieu asked my father to keep it safe or he'd tell you we weren't who we claimed to be.'

Callan flashed his teeth. 'That's not what yer father said…'

And with that, Callan had the Winstons where he wanted them: lost in their lies.

CHAPTER SIXTEEN

Aileen wasn't sure what had happened after Callan had got the confessions he'd needed. She didn't recall who had asked the doctor to come by and examine her. Nor was she sure how she'd got to bed.

All Aileen could say for certain was that she woke up sore, and disorientated – as if she was suffering from a high fever.

Isla had been there, tending to her. Her care had warmed Aileen's heart. Never had she been looked after by someone who wasn't family.

After setting a sumptuous-looking breakfast tray over Aileen's lap, Isla sat on the chair next to her bed.

'Now I don't know the whole story, but Callan told me you were in a bad state.'

'Callan told you?' Aileen's voice was raspy in the quiet room. She bent over the tray and breathed in the zesty flavour of tea.

Isla only nodded. 'He seemed concerned. He handed me a doctor's prescription. You've been asked to take pain meds and rest your back. It's nothing major that rest won't heal.'

Aileen sipped some warm tea. She ached all over, not just in her back. But that was fine, as long as the murderer had been locked away.

'What... What happened?'

Isla waved her hands. 'You fuel up first. Strength is what you need. Siobhan called. You need to speak to her.'

Aileen groaned, her joy shattering at the thought of her grandmother's wrath.

She shuffled the blanket away. 'I can't afford to be stuck in bed! I have to call Gran and beg her to let me stay on as innkeeper.'

'Why do you think she'd let you go?'

'There was a murder here – two of them – on my watch!'

Isla stared at her pointedly. 'You didn't commit them.'

All Aileen did was huff like a child.

'I think Siobhan will be proud of you. You held it together and helped solve the murders too.'

At Aileen's stubborn eye roll, Isla smirked. 'Besides, I'd love to know how you almost dislocated Cook's you know what.'

That made Aileen's eyes swell like saucers. 'What?'

'It's the talk of the town. How Dachaigh's innkeeper doesn't take well to murderous guests.'

Isla guffawed loudly, her body shaking with laugher.

Just then Aileen heard the front door open. Heavy footsteps travelled up the stairs and Callan appeared, looking haggard. He had dark circles under his eyes, and the usual smirk was missing from his face.

Aileen smiled in greeting, trying her best to keep that blush from tainting her cheeks.

It was hard to forget the look he'd given her when he'd put his hand in hers.

Callan cleared his throat. 'Just wanted to say, it's all done.'

Isla laughed at the state of him. 'You look knackered!'

'I need some shut-eye soon,' he confessed.

'I'll fix you breakfast,' Isla piped up. 'Then I can hear all about it.'

WHEN THEY'D ALL SETTLED BACK IN AILEEN'S ROOM ONCE more, Isla urged Aileen to tell her what had taken place last night.

Callan interjected, 'Isla! She can barely talk. Cook tried to strangle her last night!'

But Isla wanted the whole scoop. She turned on Callan. 'You go on then.'

He sighed but did as she asked. 'I got scraps of information from all of my three interviews. They each owned the murder weapons: the dagger as well as the belt. However, Beaulieu couldn't have killed Susan. He's too short to have tied her up like that. As for Legrand, he's far too concerned for his reputation. And he's never dealt with Susan or Dave before. Percy Winston did indeed possess the dagger but his son had sold it through the dark web. So they didn't know who they'd sold it to. Besides, it would have been foolhardy to leave behind evidence that could implicate them. Leaving it at the scene would make it easy to catch them. All the evidence suggested the first murder had been planned beforehand. But it wasn't.'

Aileen sat up, wincing at the pain, but managed to hiss out, 'What do you mean? John knew what he was doing; so did Martha. I—' The rest of it was lost in a fit of coughing.

'Oh, you poor thing. Here, sip warm water.' Isla's motherly side was shining through.

Callan continued, 'The morning I saw Martha and Dave Smith, he was threatening her or at least accusing her of something.'

Isla raised a surprised eyebrow.

Aileen paused. She hadn't figured this piece of the puzzle out!

Callan merely shrugged. 'Martha confessed. John Cook's a cousin, but they were close. He was the one person in her family that Martha kept in touch with. He never liked Martha's husband.

'Their marriage – Dave's and Martha's – wasn't a farce. They are married, albeit under different names. But lately, Dave had turned violent. You see, he knew Martha had saved some old trinkets from each of their previous identities, a sentimental thing. And he'd figured out that she'd kept in touch with John Cook. He thought these habits could land him in trouble. He did his job and, like a chameleon, changed his colours regularly so no one could ever find him. But his wife wasn't that good at shifting gears. He threatened to leave her before the hustle went through.'

Aileen sighed. She knew this part. 'I figured out I was being subjected to a grift of sorts.'

The breeze picked up, blowing refreshing air into the room. Clouds splattered the sky but it felt tranquil, like the calm after a storm.

Callan cleared his throat. 'All ten guests were here for Siobhan's ring. They'd initially thought all the diamonds were still at the inn. But it was just the ring.'

Isla's eyes were like saucers. 'All ten? Way to go, Aileen!' She chuckled at her friend.

'The idea was that John and Susan would take the ring. John had recently run into money trouble, and Susan was blackmailing him. Apparently, they'd butted heads over a case few months before where Cook had agreed to plant evidence and help a woman who wanted to swindle her husband out of money. Susan knew about it and decided to use a similar tactic.'

'That's horrible,' Aileen told Callan. 'All those women who've been wronged and there's a rotten vegetable in the pile who's just in it for the money.'

'Cook deserves what he got!' Isla said firmly. For the first time, Aileen saw her friend flush with rage.

Callan continued before both the ladies in front of him combusted. 'Well, Martha and Samantha were to pick your pocket for the keys, since you carried them wherever you went. Beaulieu and Legrand would then assess the ring to make sure it was truly a diamond, and Dave would sell it on the black-market. Everyone would get a hefty commission from the trade.'

'What about the rest of the Winstons?' Isla wanted to know.

'Easy – they'd sell a duplicate ring in their gallery. Beaulieu would help him craft the perfect one, so nobody would question its authenticity before it was too late. After all, Beaulieu is a geologist. Once sold, they'd pocket the money and disappear.'

Aileen couldn't believe this! They had a plan to make double the money with one diamond ring! Crooks!

'So when Dave told Martha he was leaving, she wanted a piece of the pie. If he left her before they sold the ring, she'd lose out on a big deal. So she approached John. He was more than happy to do away with Dave. He thought they could sell the ring with or without him. He could do with the extra money a lack of commission for Dave would save.'

Callan clicked his tongue. 'John had come prepared. I think he was planning to do away with Susan whether they got the ring or not.'

'The bastard!' Isla rubbed her hands together aggressively.

Callan let out a long breath. 'Loch Fuar is the perfect place to hide a body – we don't have the resources to search the entire landscape – and no one would know Susan was gone until he got back to London. Given their history, people would probably have just assumed they'd split up. If he'd stuck to that plan rather than all the theatrics, he might've got away with it.'

Isla raised her hand. 'But how did John steal the diamond belt?'

Callan grinned at Aileen. 'John hacked into Legrand and Beaulieu's computer just like Aileen had. They planned to sound the false alarm that night, wasn't it? John was prepared. He stole the belt when Legrand and Beaulieu vacated their room. A belt's easy to hide under your t-shirt. Isn't it, Aileen?'

Aileen groaned despite Callan's comment. She'd reached the same conclusions as he had. But getting down to the facts seemed harder. Spouses killing spouses! What had happened to love?

CALLAN STUDIED AILEEN. SHE APPEARED BETTER THAN SHE had last night. At least her eyes were clear. Yesterday she'd seemed dazed as if she might be overcome with emotion any moment. Perhaps she'd been in deep shock.

Now he wanted to know how she'd known it was John and Martha.

Aileen explained, 'I was just thinking. I knew the answer was right there. So I wrote it all down. I had so many questions. Before dinner, Martha enquired about the bread. That got me thinking about her alibi for the second murder.'

Aileen squinted. 'She'd been with Anne, talking about baking bread – she'd said they both had a passion for it. But Martha had declared her shortcomings in the kitchen, so between that and her reluctance to speak about the bread last night, something didn't add up. And when I called the women's shelter I spoke to them about signs of domestic violence and then I remembered Martha had shown those same signs. She'd flinched the night Dave came down to dinner and sat beside her. The morning they'd argued, she seemed lost. And the day they arrived? Their entrance was too flamboyant for a couple who'd been married that long! They were acting like newlyweds.'

'And ye know about actors?' Callan retorted.

'I do! I know the way executives act when you find an expense that shouldn't have been incurred.' Aileen smiled shrewdly. 'As for Susan, she didn't seem like a gullible person. She worked with women who suffered abuse. She'd have her back up, wouldn't she? And a strong nose for anyone suspicious. So how would she consume a sleeping drug if she was vigilant?'

As if driving the point home, she pointed her finger in the air. 'The only person she'd trust was her partner. Sure, they weren't seeing eye to eye, but she didn't think he'd dare kill her. She thought he still loved her. That was her downfall.'

Isla nodded, digesting it all.

'Why did he put himself in jeopardy by killing her? I

get it was his plan but after the first murder... How could he have thought he'd get away with it?'

Callan flashed his teeth. 'She was demanding money he didn't have. And she suspected he'd killed Dave. She freely admitted she couldn't account for his presence in the room all night. She went to sleep before he did. But she knew he didn't steal the ring. He couldn't have because the safe was in Aileen's bedroom and Aileen was sleeping in there. He couldn't raise suspicion by sneaking into her chambers that night. So when Dave turned up dead, and John hadn't been in bed, Susan knew who'd killed him. It gave her an excellent opportunity to press for more money.'

'John Cook had a partner after his own heart.'

'Looks like that.' Callan shrugged, huffing out a breath.

All three lapsed into silence, contemplating the sinister games that had shaken Dachaigh in the recent days.

'So how did you know Anne had the ring?'

'Percy kept an eye out – that's why he was in his room the entire night. Father and son had decided to acquire the ring. He saw Susan leave, then made sure Beaulieu and Legrand never left their rooms. Anne had the job of leading Martha Smith downstairs. She also encouraged John to join them. So Percy didn't think twice when he saw John leave his room. Instead, he informed his son that the scene was clear to move in.'

'To steal the ring from John?' Isla asked. She was sitting on the edge of her chair.

'Of course! John and Susan had already taken it from Aileen's safe. That was the original plan after all.'

Aileen cleared her throat. 'I never got that part — when did they get the ring?'

Callan chuckled, 'We figured Susan and Samantha could've slashed your car tyres.'

'Aye.'

'From the confessions, I made out that Anne and Samantha Grant slashed your car tyres after Samantha and Susan Knight made sure everyone had gone to that vendor meeting.'

Aileen nodded, 'That's when John and Susan stole the ring?'

'Aye.'

Isla shuffled to the edge of her seat. 'And when the lights went out? Is that when John killed Susan?' she asked.

Callan supplied her with the answers. 'No, that was Percy's idea. He didn't trust his fellow grifters. He fought with his son when he saw the blade that killed Dave. But he knew for certain Jake couldn't have killed Susan because he was busy stealing the ring from their room. All Percy then had to do was warn Jake if John or Susan returned. Jake cut the lights. That would mean he could return to his room without being seen.'

Aileen made a tsk sound. 'And if he was about, there was a perfectly reasonable explanation – the lights had gone off.'

Isla made a noise in her throat. 'The four of them were that sure they'd be allowed to leave without raising suspicion?'

'Apparently… Anne was the most innocent of the lot. Jake gave her the ring and asked her to wear it around her neck. That way they could smuggle it out of the inn. She was the last person on my suspect list as well.'

When Aileen raised a mocking eyebrow, Callan quickly added, 'Not counting you!'

That brought some laughter after their dreary talk.

The day didn't bear any melancholy though; nature was in a mood to rejoice.

It was a pleasant day. The sun made the entire landscape come alive with spring colours and Loch Fuar glittered with life in the distance.

Callan rubbed his eyes. He looked like all he wanted was to collapse into bed, but instead, he huffed, snorted and turned to Aileen. 'I believe I owe you a date.'

Aileen waved her hands. 'Oh, that's okay! Between us, we can assume it's done.'

Callan shook his head. 'Rory's a traitor. He'll rat me out to Siobhan. And to be honest, she's one woman I refuse to cross.'

Aileen's eyes crinkled. Callan respected her gran. In fact, everyone in town did.

'Maybe after the doctor gives you the all-clear, we'll grab dinner or something.' Callan stuffed his hands into his pockets as if they might give him away. Surely he wasn't nervous? It was just dinner.

'Sure.' Aileen tried a casual smile.

ISLA'S GAZE FLITTERED BETWEEN THE TWO. THIS COULD BE interesting, she thought.

Oh Siobhan, you intelligent woman.

Isla couldn't wait to see what happened next.

Turn the page to read the next adventure in Aileen and Callan's life

WHEN EYES DON'T LIE

The angry sky spoke of violent storms and worrying nights. Night had descended with an inky darkness—a bit too early for summer—thanks to the overcast sky.

She approached the windows in her kitchen and peered out.

What was that?

Something flashed out in the dark. The beam flickered, a beckoning light in the dense blackness of the night. It sparkled and remained bright.

Who was out there? Was someone stranded in this treacherous weather? In Loch Fuar, no one was foolish enough to tread the rocky Highlands this late in the evening. Perhaps she could bring the lost people to safety.

Tugging on her jacket, Aileen wrenched open the door, preparing herself.

A breeze as freezing as the Antarctic blew into the inn laced with the metallic mucky earth.

Oh Lord, was a person out there in this harsh weather? Like a good Samaritan, she called out. 'Anyone there?'

The only answer was the gushing wind with thick droplets of rain.

Aileen licked her dry lips. Perhaps she should just stay indoors, after all, it was warm and dry in here. The moonless night cried like a wolf, causing goosebumps to rise over her skin.

Placing a foot back indoors, Aileen desperately tried shutting the door when she heard herself. Was she *afraid* to step out?

No. No, she wasn't.

Carefully locking the door behind her, Aileen braved the weather, calling out again.

This time, the response was pelting raindrops that crashed over her in a flurry, their wet earthy taste leaving her mouth bitter.

She muttered a curse and shuffled backwards when the light in the distance stopped, flickered, and stilled.

Was someone playing games? Trying to scare her? Or were they young lads, out on a night like this undoubtedly not in their senses?

What day was it? It didn't take her mind long to answer: Saturday.

Saturday night and young lads not in their senses, those two were strongly correlated.

This time she huffed, anger quickly replacing fear. As a young adult, Aileen never had the urge to spend her time 'socialising'. She'd rather be with her books: fiction, non-fiction, or old ledgers.

That's the reason you're all alone with less than adequate social skills.

Dismissing the usual back and forth between her inner critique and her head, she trudged towards the light.

She *was* confident, Aileen reassured herself.

Thank goodness for the plastic torch clutched tightly

in her grasp. She'd learnt this important lesson since coming down to Loch Fuar: nights were dark with no streetlights. Using the torch on your phone meant the phone could die.

Thus, a physical torch it was.

The downpour miffed Aileen, knowing what a mess her boots would be, but she slogged on. After a while of questioning if she was being a fool, Aileen surveyed the treacherous landscape in this blasphemous weather. At least she wasn't tipsy like the lads in the distance undeniably were. And she was well-equipped too. There seemed to be no ditches that could hurt her… Severely, anyway.

Aileen hunched, drawing her jacket tighter around herself to retain what little warmth she had. Her jeans were completely soaked!

After dragging her feet through the dirt for a while, Aileen lost track of time. She tried her best to walk faster, but the damp earth and exertion made her footsteps sloppy, especially when the wind joined in with the vicious dance of the rain.

What kept her pushing forward was the light. It had flickered again. She was irrefutably curious.

Aileen desperately tried not to swallow the rainwater that assaulted her mouth. The taste reminding her of iron, bitter and metallic. Her only reprieve was the light, which blazed brighter as she approached it.

After a while, Aileen cleared the bushes—or what she thought were bushes—pushing past them only to emerge on a landing of sorts.

An unnatural guttural cry from above made Aileen's knees go weak and her heart raced.

Golly!

She clasped her wet wrinkled fingers together, as if in prayer. Squinting, Aileen flicked the dripping moisture from her tired eyes. Right in front of her was a small cottage!

That's where the light was coming from!

She let out a soft chuckle. Aileen had never noticed this cottage before. And judging by the crack in its roof, the place seemed neglected. It was a surprise it had any electricity at all. Surely it housed stranded people. The cottage could crumble at any moment on a good day. It certainly couldn't withstand this storm.

With best wishes in her heart, Aileen walked up to the door and called out. But her voice was lost to the otherworldly calls which assaulted her ears.

Aileen frowned at the slightly ajar door.

Who'd leave the door hanging open in this blasted weather? Perhaps it wouldn't close…

She let it go; she was overthinking. As usual. Using all the breath in her lungs she called out again, Aileen's fear was long forgotten, hoping to help someone. Despite her shouts, she was met with silence.

Once again Aileen wiped the rainwater from her eyes. Her hands had gone pale and shivered. She licked her lips. What if this was some elaborate scheme to harm her?

This is Loch Fuar, Aileen! Adventurous, Courageous!

With one hand on the slippery torch, Aileen steeled herself. A moment later, she pulled the rough wooden door open. 'Hell-'

Her words died in her mouth and what came out was a terrifying scream. Her pruney hands shook, and legs trembled. Her throat burned with bile and she couldn't breathe.

Right in the centre of the room, just above where a wooden beam ran across the ceiling, a rope dangled.

And on that rope hung a ghost. White limbs attached to a blonde head tumbled over onto a shoulder, clad in a dirty milky dress.

Lightning struck, illuminating the dangling body.

A freezing breeze tickled Aileen's clenched fists and played with the murky hem of the corpse's dress.

The swaying feet were almost blue…

Aileen's shaky hands pressed the soft fabric of her coat that kept her warm… Alive. A repulsive, rancid reek tugged at her gut.

Dead. The dangling woman was surely dead.

Read 'When Eyes Don't Lie'
OR
Purchase Books 1-6 in a Collection Boxset
Please note: The Collection is not available on Amazon

Available at all retailers and in libraries

READ THE EXCLUSIVE NOVELLA

**When a storm cuts off the tiny town of Loch Fuar
from the rest of the world, a murderer strikes.
And it's someone among them.**

Download your free copy: Shanafrost.com/exclusivenovella

AUTHOR'S NOTE

Dear Reader,

Thank You from the bottom of my heart for taking this tumultuous journey with Aileen and Callan. Writing this debut novel has been one of the most cathartic yet gut-churning experiences in my life. No one ever said writing a novel was easy:)

If you'd like to have a chat about this book or have any questions or suggestions, please write to me at author@shanafrost.com.

I would be very grateful if you could also leave a review for this book. Your review helps an independent author like me reach new readers. If you've never written a review before, you don't need to write a long literary essay, just a sentence or two on your preferred retailer store is perfect. And if you have the time, please also leave a review on Goodreads and/or Bookbub as well. Thank you.

As I write this note, I cannot recall when the idea for 'When Murder Comes Home' came to mind, but I know that the character of Aileen Mackinnon didn't become my closest friend overnight; she revealed herself as I jotted this story down, bit by bit.

Aileen's self-doubt isn't something uncommon. Many of us struggle with it most of our lives. Self-doubt often keeps us from achieving our full potential, or in Aileen's words, it makes us settle for a 'risk-less' life. Of course, kicking a murderer in his 'you know what' won't resolve self-doubt overnight. But here's to hoping she'll overcome it eventually!

Our favourite bloke, Callan Cameron isn't uncomplicated either, but his cursing surely made the entire experience fun to write. Somehow, it's easy to see these two pick fights, it's so entertaining.

But I must confess, writing a novel is not a lone wolf's job. Thus, there are a few people I need to thank.

Firstly, my alpha reader and my meticulous cousin Sharika: thank you for reading the raw draft of this novel.

Thank You to my cousin Neeraja whose detailed comments for improvements in the penultimate draft made this novel so much better.

A big Thank You to my copyeditor, Laura Kincaid who answered my never-ending questions about the self-publishing world and reassured me in times of self-doubt (ironic isn't it, the characters you birth). Her detailed inputs have made me a better writer and this novel, way richer.

To all my beta readers: Rohan, Willow, Isha and my dear Aunt—Thank You!

And lastly, I cannot ignore the two people without whom this book or my flair for writing would've never come to light: my parents. Thank You for your unconditional support in all my ventures. For where would I be if you didn't believe in me?

Wow, this note was really hard to write, harder than a novel.

So, I'll take a bow now. It's time to retreat to my writing den to scribble the next adventure. I can't let Aileen and Callan's lives be dull any longer, can I?

See ye soon,

Shana

ABOUT THE AUTHOR

Shana Frost writes romantic mysteries as dramatic as the Scottish Highlands that inspire her. In every book, Shana shares the values she truly believes in: hope, justice, and love. Throughout her novels, you'll encounter a variety of characters—be their gender, ethnicity, disabilities, beliefs—all sharing their unique stories.

Always infused with a wee dram of the Scottish landscape and culture, Shana's stories take readers from Glasgow's gritty streets to the enigmatic Highlands. She promises that when reading her stories, you'll be at the edge of your seat, falling deeper in love with the characters.

To be enveloped in the world of Scottish romantic mysteries, visit Shana's home on the web at
Shanafrost.com

THANK YOU!

Thanks for reading thus far. I've got a surprise for you!

What was Aileen and Callan's life like before murder came home?

Click here or type this URL in your browser to find out: **Shanafrost.com/a&c**

Made in the USA
Middletown, DE
21 September 2024

61254842R00144